Nimmer

THE DARK CHILD

ROMEO VEGA

Copyright © 2024 Romeo Vega
All rights reserved
First Edition

PAGE PUBLISHING
Conneaut Lake, PA

First originally published by
Page Publishing 2024

ISBN 979-8-89553-061-0 (pbk)
ISBN 979-8-89553-076-4 (digital)

Printed in the United States of America

CHAPTER I

THE CREATORS

There is always a flaw in the system.
In this universe, God herself
happens to be one of them.

At the beginning of time, in the first moments of the universe, and the beginning stages of matter, the god of this universe, Asherah, had spawned all alone in total darkness. She began to wake in the universe even when it was filled with nothingness, with the total absence of life and death. There were no stars, no planets, and no ingredients to make life itself. With a swift motion of her hand, she built a throne of white; from there she cast a castle with rooms. Here she named her space the Crystal

City, the dome of creation. She sat in her throne room alone, and after a long rotation, she made the decision to create. And with a thought of her own, she formed an entity of light beyond human but still had features. The next thing she knew, she not only had one creation, but also seven gods of all importance for sustainability had spawned. They gathered around her, and she was the one to speak. "My dear leaders, I ask for your help to think of a unified universe."

They all stood and pondered on her request. The God of *Healing* had a question. "What grants us the right to be worthy?" They looked at Asherah collectively, and she stood still with fear but calmness in herself.

She took a moment to answer because even she didn't know what made her important. "All of you are your gods. You govern the laws and reasons of how this universe operates. All of you are important because you are the first ones here with me. You all can't be replaced." They cheered, and with a motion from their minds, they too built their thrones next to one another. And all together they ruled. Asherah gathered the gods around a table and settled on a discussion about the importance of balance.

"You mean a balance of good and evil?" God of *Power* said.

"No, I'm talking about death, and that if life itself doesn't come to an end, then there would be no difference between us gods and the creations we give the privilege to feel. They will eventually have to die." Everyone paused in silence, for they didn't know what to say about letting their creations die off.

One opinion of disapproval was shouted across the room from the God of *Healing*. "I shall not let my sons and daughters be sent to an unknown place, nor will they have to come to an end!"

A room of uproars erupted with questions of the afterlife. "Perhaps when they leave the mortal world, they can come here and stay with us for all eternity," the God of *Universal Travel* had spoken and led with her open arms.

God of *Worlds* said, "What if they don't want to come to see us when they die?" And more began to speak with questions about their role as gods.

"Would they still have a choice in their journey in the afterlife? Should we govern them to make the correct decisions when they die?" asked the God of *Power*.

An argument among the God of *Destruction* was, "Of course they will have to choose. This is the balance we are talking about. I say our creations have an ending, but let it be their final destination."

An unspoken god had a statement to declare; it was the God of *Stars*. "I believe that our creations should be born free, and at the end of their lives, they be set free, such envy we aspire. Of course, we will have a hand in their lives but not too much. They will still have to survive without our power of control. Who else believes freedom is every living creature's right?"

The God of *Worlds* asked, "Wait a moment. What will we do with the ones who take their life. Do they still have freedom even if they take the one gift they are entitled to?" None had an obligation to answer, but all did ponder on the question of, most importantly, why such a creature should be broken to the point of self-destruction.

NIMMER

The God of *Love* had to share her thoughts on this discussion. "Pain must come before love, and I will always cherish my beloved children, broken or fixed, sad or mad, dead or alive. I recommend they be treated the same as the others who encounter death."

That was settled, but not the procedure of making the universe. "If creatures of all kinds have the right to be free, then we have no say in what they must choose. We can only give them options for them, and from there on, they can choose what they would like to do. We mustn't turn against each other, it's our responsibility to take care of our children and have a balanced union," Asherah stated with her hands attached. She stood still and centered and continued the process. "All those in favor of setting up an afterlife for our creations?" All raised their hands, and the motion was passed. In the center of the table, a growing ball of light spawned. It grew and grew till the girth of the ball had reached both sides of the rectangle table. It stopped and gently lifted into the space above to be soaked into the sky, which became the place of afterlife. Then suddenly, a figure of black, an entity of shape-shifting form, appeared. This was Death itself, for it held control over this domain and had all the combined power of the other gods.

Whatever the creature chooses, they will be sent here to Death to send them to wherever they want to go. They could spend their time with the gods for all eternity, or if they chose to be a ghostly figure, they would be sent back but not seen, only felt. And in a last-minute breath, it was added that they could do neither and be one with the universe. Death would have souls in its pocket if they chose this path.

Death vanished in smoke, and the gods were left to their own. Then all left to explore and add their memorable monuments, such as the God of *Worlds* placing his many little color-filled planets. There was one he didn't mean to place: a dark-blue planet with power within. Also, the God of *Stars* added his beautiful cosmic rays everywhere so that the gods could see in the dark, such as a state that holds power. The God of *Destruction* asked cursed questions: "If the living must die, does that mean there must be evil in the universe to take those lives?" They all journeyed back to the table of light after they had set their creations. Asherah brought them all in a hug and then stood back to give her a topic of conversation.

She looked down at the floor and sighed with relief. "We must hold another discussion."

The testified God of *Healing* had a say. "Evil? Isn't it you who brings evil into our dome of power!" Everyone was on guard because each one was against the other.

The God of *Stars* calmed them. "Let's be civil here. We can all agree that this doesn't have to come down to war." Tension between the gods arose as some were siding for violence.

The God of *Worlds* loudly stated, "I will not have my lands poisoned by whatever corruptness you spawn!" Asherah commanded that they not yell at one another.

There was a moment of silence, then a gentle and confident voice came from the God of *Love*. "With what death brings, so must be the cause of such power to take life. This is the important discussion of our very existence. There must be a balance of both good and evil."

The God of *Universal Travel*, who just now arrived, said, "What is the purpose of this conversation? I have been traveling and doing my own business." A demonstration appeared above them all—a show of balance from both life and death and the effects of good and bad in the universe. There was a complete collapse of just goodness and then death.

Asherah spoke to end the demonstration. "Can't you see? Without evil, there won't be a balance, and soon enough our existence will fade."

All stood to think, but out of the thoughts, the God of *Power* voiced his question. "What kind of evil? Do you suppose we call upon a calamity?"

Asherah agreed then continued, "Here's what the motion is. Once a rotation, a great evil will have to spawn, and here this calamity will take lives and even out the odds of good and bad. Heroes of courage and strength of both mind and muscle will destroy this calamity till the next time it comes again."

Not all saw eye to eye; some had some comments and concerns. The God of *Healing* had a question: "And if these heroes can't kill the evil?"

Asherah responded with the devastating message. "Then everything will come to an end. It will first consume *Power* and then leave the last *Star* so that no more *Sparklights* spawn."

The God of *Power*, with the same idea as the rest, asked "Are we able to fight back this evil? For example, if our heroes are in desperate need of help, could we help them?"

Asherah stood and pondered his question, and then she answered with a deal. "If we can all agree to this motion, then we will have to make rules—seven unbroken laws that set this calamity." A moment of acceptance from all gods came with a long silence. They looked at each other, a wave of knowledge flowing within themselves. They all understood the importance of this motion. One by one they raised their hands, and one was left.

The God of *Worlds* had a question, for all they needed was his vote. "Can we build a weapon so that every time this evil comes, we can just use it?"

Asherah disagreed with it. "Then what purpose does our creation serve? If we as gods do the heavy lifting, then what life is that for the immortal?" The God of *Worlds* sat in silence because he answered the question in his head. Thus with his question out of the way, he voted.

Asherah creates the sacred text written on the walls behind their thrones. Here she wrote from top to bottom. Then from around their thrones came a black cloud, a single crack leaking like black blood. This was calamity; a motion was cast from there forward that Asherah would have to call upon a great calamity as a test for who will be the beholder. The gods collectively knew that there had to be a balance between good and evil. It's the great wisdom: to have light, you must have darkness first. By this blessing set in time, in a rotation, there would be a great danger to come.

NIMMER

The Foundation

1. Gods can help out our dear heroes either in the form of a weapon or by giving courage. They must not tell the future or place themselves as selfless as the heroes.
2. Death itself cannot warn immortal life or demigods before calamity occurs.
3. When the warrior or warriors conquer the calamity, they must set their duty as that and be ready for the next if necessary.
4. No team larger than four can defeat calamity.
5. Demigods will be the main hunted life-form in the universe. After they are gone, immortals will be next.
6. The calamity has one mission and will forever hold one mission. That is to eliminate the demigods of the universe and take all life away.
7. If the calamity has won, then there will be no life as good as I have created that will ever exist.

CHAPTER II

THE SIX CHILDREN AND THE BURNING ROCK MADE UP OF POWER

A while had passed since these rules were set. Death would do his own business as usual, and the gods grew to not have a problem with the souls he would take. He was the odd one out. Many of the gods became one with the creations—living among them, taking care of them, and falling in love. This occurred many times with all of the gods. They were falling for mortals and giving birth to a new creation: demigods. The God of *Stars* had the most powerful child out of the bunch. For the power their parents held transpired to the offspring. The God of

Universal Travel had a special and eye-opening effect on this. Her child won't be born till long after this story takes place. The God of *Destruction*, with no passion to cause great destruction. His child would be one of the first demigods born in the year 1,000. It was on his twelfth birthday that his father knew he didn't want to cause harm to others, so he gifted a flower to a criminal in a cage as a sign of peace. The God of *Destruction* didn't take this so easily, but days after, he would come to accept his son and always remind him of what kind of potential he held.

The power to create not just worlds with life but moons as well is a great power in itself, and therefore the God of *Worlds* was probably the second strongest god, along with his child that was born not too long ago from when he met the love of his life. The child born from the God of *Worlds* grew up with no mother, and there came an illness that swept away most of the population they lived on. The God of *Worlds* couldn't do anything to stop Death in his path to taking her. As Death arrived to take the soul of his beloved wife, the God of *Worlds* begged for him not to take her. He wept and cried as he looked into Death's eyes and saw no remorse or shame in what he had done right in front of him.

The child, just a few months old, lay in a crib across the hall from Death; and when he had left, the God of *Worlds*, alone in sorrow and distraught, sat in the very room where his wife had been taken. The God of *Worlds* made it his mission to make sure Death never came for his son. So when the boy was old enough (fourteen years old), his father told him what kind of powers he held within himself and that he expected greatness from him. "You can create worlds, my son. I want you to crush your enemies with rocks the size of planets. Never let Death get close to you, no matter what."

The God of *Healing* had a child too, with a man who had no powers of any kind but still hit with his hands as if he held some sort of authority over the very God of *Healing*. She was a self-repairing medic for most of her love life. She sometimes blamed the God of *Love* for the many wounds she had suffered from the hands of beating men. "Why do you hate me!" she cried at the God of *Love* whenever they would meet in the heavens.

NIMMER

"The pain builds and strengthens your powers to heal. I do not act on my actions for entertainment purposes. I'm sorry, but it's a sacrifice I have to risk taking."

She had gone back to her violent husband and knew that her child must not end up like her. So one sunny glorious morning, the God of *Healing* woke her husband up and asked if he wanted breakfast. He said yes with a tone of resentment. She had cooked him a meal of poisoned potatoes and lovely green beans. Death knew what she was doing, and with no comment, he came to the kitchen to watch. The God of *Healing* looked at Death with eyes of rage and preparation. He looked back and said, "Glorious morning, isn't it?"

She scoffed and replied, "Don't tell anyone you saw me do this." The husband came down the stairs with the footsteps of a monster. Even Death couldn't wait to snatch him like a good turkey leg for dinner. He waited in the kitchen, unseen by the mortal husband.

She said the usual "morning" and the "sleep well?" His toxic habit of not listening enraged her even more, but all he had to do was take a bite and he'd be gone. Then moments after he took two to three bites, he turned red; and second by second, he lost each feeling in his limbs. Death collected his soul and vanished.

The little girl had one parent, and it was her god of a mother. She came to the age of sixteen, and here she learned the importance of both healing oneself and others. She'd never be told about her abusive father or the consequences of his actions. Instead, it was left to her mother to make a fabricated lie, and along with that lie, it grew both women's power, increasing the healing rate and being adjustable to each organism. Last but not least, the demigod of *Love* was the weakest, not physically, but what she could offer was very limited. She would not be helpful in a team fight, you could say. Her backstory won't be all that bad when she comes into her own.

While the others had a basic understanding and premise of power, nothing compares to what Xanthia had. Her father was the God of *Stars*, and she was a team leader and the most powerful demigod out of all the others. Her mother was a champion of combat and strength, and her home planet was one of the most important and impactful out of the others too. It was called Knox (the first letter is silent, so it's pronounced "nox"). They had one of the most valuable ores in the universe, gifted to them by the God of *Worlds* because they were both good friends. Xanthia's family became an extremely wealthy family and even took full control of the planet they lived on. It didn't matter if one or two nations had already been declared and should not be allied with anyone; the most powerful god was not in the mood for ignorance and future war with the same people. So on a night of peace, the God of *Stars* rose from his bed, went through a window, and flew to the nation that was on the opposite side of the planet, with the same people that wouldn't agree to calibration.

He found where the leader had lived, stalking like a vulture in the air where no one could see him. It had been later in the day when the sun was at its peak. Guards had been on patrol. It wasn't a problem for him. He positioned his hand at the sun then heightened the heat from the star to burn and set fire to the weapons and flesh of the guards. In a matter of minutes, the emperor and his followers panicked, and the rocks they walked on became an extremely scorching lava surface. They screamed for mercy, but he had no remorse for his actions. In the last moments of the rebel leader, the pyromaniac went down to the barely alive creature, stood over the leader, and said, "Such a shame."

Death had been hiding in sight but stood behind the God of *Stars* till he was spotted. "All these people are yours. Have fun, champ."

Death was not amused by the comment. He replied, "You gods are ruthless with the powers you were given."

The God of *Stars*, with a smirk on his face while looking at Death, flew off as if he was not the cause of the 150 burnt unrecognizable bodies that lay before him. He had no choice but to collect the souls of ash that seemed to die from doomsday. Speaking of doomsday, the God of *Power* had his plans of racking up a kill count. He could never imagine falling in love with a mortal on a planet not fit for royalty. The God of *Power* thought very highly of himself. Deep down he was angry at the fact that he wasn't the most powerful god, even becoming somewhat enemies with the God of *Stars*. He knew as soon as the first star was born that he could never have such a great impact on the universe. So he thought of a plan to create an offspring that would take the powers of the other demigods and then give all this power to him, but it would come with a sacrifice of taking away his creation for the outcome of being the most powerful entity.

He didn't care. He thought of himself and only him. He was filled with narcissistic tendencies and madness. So the God of *Power* saw fit to add a margin of error in these writings of light. He created an asteroid that contained a powerful being called Yetzer, the child of fire, a demigod of *Power*. He hid Yetzer in a swirling pool of ring-like rocks, behind a star unnoticed by the God of *Stars*. He kneeled and placed his antihero. Technically this was his child even if he didn't fall for a mortal. He created a child with such determination to kill and with no recognizable emotions or values at heart.

"There you shall stay until I call upon your presence of destruction. Yetzer, destroy every demigod there is. And make me more powerful than God." Unfortunately, he didn't know that this star would die sooner. A bit further away from the belt of rocks stayed a planet of dark blue, a glittery, living pulse-blue planet. Yetzer was not born here, for when the star lost its ability to survive, its own heat and cosmic energy got absorbed into Yetzer's body of rock. When that star let out its final blow of scream-like life, the belt broke into pieces like broken glass on the floor, and Yetzer was sent off into space at fast speeds—so fast not a single god could catch him. They wouldn't have thought about stopping the future. A bright blood-red tail from the flying rock crossed many lives, but at the end of its journey, it crashed on a planet. The sand oozed into the pod. It healed the wounds Yetzer had sustained when the blast hit him. He wasn't awake, but he could feel the healing process and the power within the planet.

Dark-blue glitter cosmic dust—this was Nimmer. It was not a person, not an action, not a weapon, but a very powerful force of light and darkness combined. It was the planet itself—the sand, the planet's core, and the environment. When it came in contact with any living organism, the power

NIMMER

within the planet would be in the hands of the beholder. The power/Nimmer ranged from matter manipulation to self-destruction. Yetzer was dormant, holding its rightful place on Nimmer, with the rumbling of the destroyer. The shell cracked and busted open a power wave of flames. It was a signal to the nearest demigod that was a planet away, almost like it was destiny to create a hero from Yetzer's actions. In this solar system on the edge of the universe, not only did it keep home to a star and four planets all with life but also the demigod of *Love.*

CHAPTER III

LIGHT PINK VERSUS DARK RED

The planet the demigod of *Love* lived on was, from the start, gray and dull, but her mother went there and made it her mission to make it a beautiful, better place for the future people who would come to live there. This planet was unique in its way, even though it was gray and much of a ghost town; it had a beautiful secret of history. This planet had crystals in its core and a variety of colors with different properties they held. The God of *Love* was thankful for the opportunity of the crystals. They drilled away at the land they stood on with the help of the God of *Destruction* destroying what lay before them while at the same time creating a new coat of land. It was a forgotten world that was dancing alone at the edge of the universe.

The God of *Worlds* came down and asked if the God of *Love* needed help rebuilding her very own home. She said yes along with a few requests. "Can you make two moons for me?"

He replied, "As you wish." From the ground he picked up two of the tiniest pebbles and tossed them both into space, just far enough away from the planet they sat, then he raised his hand in the air and he increased the size of the pebbles from little rocks to the size of moons. The view was magnificent to watch. All three gods stood together to see the moons dancing around the planet. He could change the size of both moons with no sweat or strain from his body.

"Perfect?" he said.

The God of *Love* saw her plans with the planet. "Just as they were meant to be. Thank you so much for your help," she said to both gods who helped her with building her planet. The gods left to her build her kingdom, which she first built a shake away from where she wanted the town to be. Natives were living within the forest of darkness on the other side of the planet. One of the natives, with green feathers on his forehead and ankles, saw the God of Love and fell for her at first glance. She had stayed on the planet when she had a child whom she named Quartz. The forest of light was on the opposite side of the forest of darkness. The pink willow trees grew to the humming tunes from Quartz. She found nature to be her friend; the animals came to her with gifts and laughter. From the smallest creatures, like the three-eyed squirrel that lived under the trees, to the largest creatures, like the mysterious, ghostly, transparent horse that had been a myth to some but real to Quartz.

Quartz's mother made sure to have peace in the town, which she had built away from the natives. Not all were willing to go with her to a new world. Her first interaction with the natives was a gift. She went up to the leader of the first tribe and said, "I mean you no harm. I would like to help you all to a new world of tranquility." They understood her, but not all found her offer to be updated to their living environment. They were hunters. They made themselves spectacles of a self-made colosseum of blood and stone. The majority chose to stick with their leader, but there were about six of them who went with the God of *Love*. The leader questioned the actors of the gods that had visited them. Just as long as they didn't cause war to his people, he didn't mind sharing some of the world. The natives would live in peace for the rest of their lives; they would casualty trade with both the God of *Love* and among the rest of the planets.

Quartz lived to be fifteen years old when Yetzer was born and raised to his limitations of power on the planet Nimmer. The God of *Love* had taken notice of the planet on a day of gardening and suggested to her few cast of friends that they should explore the suspenseful world in the distance.

Meanwhile, on the dioxazine-purple planet, Yetzer had been walking around, exploring the planet's surface. There wasn't much to the planet, barely anything to call life. That is why this planet was a force to be reckoned with. All it held was power in its sand, which made the planet not inhabitable for any living creature except the ones who came into contact with the sand, meaning you would have to touch the sand to survive on the planet. But the question was, Could someone handle that much responsibility, especially on a larger scale?

Yetzer looked around and noticed that he was the only one standing. The dark-orange sun on the horizon always stayed in that same spot and never moved. The gold-pink lemonade hue appeared on his face for which he posed and bathed in the glory of solitude. He felt true happiness in this color. By the look of his black-plum skin, the color of ash, he knew by the sight of his hands that he held power. He aimed his choral arm at the sun, opening his hand; and with a scream, from his fingertips to his shoulder, his arm lit up in a ruby-red hue/glow. There was a cannon blast of Nimmer energy shot from the palm into the universe, eventually fading away into the void.

He stood for a moment, staring off into space, and then a rush of anger fueled him. He thought, *I'm alone?* He used both hands to send out blasts around his surroundings, twisting and turning around to let all his anger out, moving as if he were in battle with ghosts. But this could not sustain his anger. He noticed the sand he stood on had a ripple effect. Kneeling and touching the sand, he felt the connection. He grabbed a handful of the sand and let it fall between his fingers. He quickly learned that he could control the sand with his mind. He stood up and so did an echo of himself. It was a doppelgänger. Yetzer looked within this soulless being. Whispers oozed out from the fake lavender eyes. He hugged his ghost self for a moment but then broke apart the body just as he felt the slightest bit complete inside. Even though it was a ghost, he still had lost something and now felt alone. His anger seemed to be the core of his powers. The more he felt rage, the longer he could hold his Nimmer power in his hand. Once again, his arms were bursting in red aura. With a stomp from his foot and a thought from his mind, he created twelve walls as targets.

With blood moon blast after blood moon blast, he broke the walls of sand; and eventually, he developed a fighting spirit and style. The walls had fallen into the sand it once was. Yetzer had built his armor that matched the color of his power. It was a blacksmith's creation, but the concept came from a villain's mind. It was an all-black choral canvas with lava fire engraved into it, and a bright red cape that started from his right shoulder and ended on his left hip. Yetzer had customized himself into a Greek god. Since he had this power to create, he added two molten core-bladed dangers to each hip. He stood strong, not as a demigod because he fully believed that he was more than that. He looked at the glory light—the amber yellow painted on his eyesight on the horizon. Once more he felt glorious in this color.

Someone had whispered his name in the howling loneliness in the sand. He looked around, ready to kill the voice that said his name. Just as he reached for his blades, a being emerged from thin air, a warped being made from the sand, and a broken star. It was Yetzer's creator, the God of *Power*. He walked toward Yetzer, but not with open arms. Yetzer took his father as an enemy, so he tried to strike him with the four dangers on his hip, swiftly and violently grabbing and throwing the blades strategically at the head. The God of *Power* was not outsmarted, so as the dangers had gotten close, he raised his hand and disintegrated the blades one by one.

The God of *Power* was ashamed of his son's actions. He said, while standing at arm's length, "That's no way to greet your father." Yetzer spawned two more daggers in his hand, preparing to throw them. He stood defensive of this suspicious man.

"Prove to me that you are my father!" he said with a smoker's voice; he was a pirate but not of action, only tune. The hands of grace touched the sides of his face, and the weapons dissolved into the sand and fell out from his hands. Yetzer didn't shed a tear because he was too angry to feel anything else.

"You are my son, and I have come to make you powerful," his father said while looking into his brimstone eyes.

Yetzer asked how with madness in his eyes. His father said with enthusiasm, "You are going to kill every single demigod that ever had lived. Once you take their life, I need you to absorb their powers. This will make you stronger. Once you have killed all the demigods in the universe, meet me back here so I can take the powers you have." Yetzer seemed a little uneasy about his father's plan. The God of *Power* had tried his best to manipulate his son into believing he was the good guy. In the end, Yetzer was willing to gain power even if he didn't understand the gravity of his father's plan.

"Who do I kill first, Father?" There was a maniacal look in his noir eyes and facial expression.

The God of *Power* saw it fit for Yetzer to go from the weakest demigod and the closest one too. "I want you to kill this demigod called Quartz. She's the weakest but don't let that stop you from taking her life. Each time you do, I will talk to you through your head, telling you who to go after." Yetzer grinned and accepted his newfound value in spawning Death.

Meanwhile at home with Quartz, she found herself in the light forest one day, running around the rocks of magic. This place was where she found her mother's power, the ability to give any loving being around her love and speed peace. The first example of her greatness was with the ghost horse of a tropical liquid, a blue four-legged beast. It was a night of wonderland brightened by the moonlight; an explorer at heart, she was.

NIMMER

The grass glowed in lime, and the leaves on the trees above her head beamed the moon's washed gray spotlight. Quartz had an infinite supply of self-love. She danced to the healing tunes of the birds and cheery fur wolf howls. The yin and yang moons danced with her and brightened her path to find her way through the thick fog where the horse lived. On the side of the defensive smoke lived a light-blue luminous pond with magnificent views that seemed a bit out of this realm. She saw in awe that frogs with silver chrome skin jumped in the water to change the color of their skin to adapt, and the fireflies of gold fire went in and out of sight.

On the other side of the pond of lapis, the pellucid horse had lay on the floor in a cave, carving the land with leaves and sheets of flowers as the soft bed. It was at rest and lived in peace till, of course, Quartz shouted in playful ignorance. The ghostly figure had crawled out and stood tall, calling out to the fireflies and other insects of the pond to come and attack Quartz. They raced after her face with unseen jaws and pacing hands, ready for scratching. Quartz had seen the wave of bugs behind the horse being released by its command. She raised her arms in an *X* shape over her head, and with a ducking manner, made herself a shield. The bugs ran into her force field that splashed the color light-rose-gold pink and soon created a half-cut dome around her. She could not feel the pressure nor harm from the bugs, for her great strength of love overpowered them all and leveled the playing field when she let out a burst of royal-rose-pink energy with a swing from both of her arms. Her first attempt at using her power was loud and shocking. She had a lot to learn about herself and what her capabilities were. The horse recognized her strength and respected her by giving away one of its rewards.

An off-white horn came from something much larger than her. It was tied to a rope with blue leaves and vines. Quartz got closer to the horse's head and rubbed and massaged its lower mouth and noise. The fireflies flew along with the rest of the bugs, coming back to celebrate the achievement Quartz had earned. She couldn't ride the horse because of its nonexistent physical presence, so they stood side by side in all cases. Quartz helped out all around the forest using her power of love to calm her fellow friends of the woods down; there would be so many altercations between the woodland creatures that she lost count.

But keeping the forest safe wasn't her only job. Her mother's village wanted to capitalize on the magical essence that was held within the bark of trees. On a day of rain, Quartz went up to her mother and demanded that they not take advantage of the magic. Somehow, even the hearts of gods can change because hers was not in a place of sympathy. Perhaps her actions in being queen had changed the way she treated others, and she forgot her vows to love others. It was a sad sight to face for her mother to ignore the pleading words, for her position changed who the God of *Love* was. She had not a heart of stone but a heart with no remorse—a heart that values the wrong things in such valuable lifetimes. The God of *Love* was not about to start a war on her daughter for standing for what is right. So she simply locked her away from the forest, in a dungeon under the house they lived in. The day before the raid on the forest, Quartz was ordered by her mother to clean the underground room, but here in the moment of trapping, the God of *Love* had put a lock on the door when shutting it. Quartz felt this rage at the acts of her mother. "How could you do this, Mother!" she yelled from her livid heart.

The God of *Love* and the rest of the village gathered in a riot hall in front and center of the lavender rain paradise. The seaside dark-blue phoenix horse knew something was wrong considering Quartz didn't show up at her normal time. The spirit came to the edge of the woods to see the village ready to charge, holding fireballs and blades. He ran back in fear, warning the creatures to hide or to start running with him as well. There was a shore a few miles away from the magnificent trees, but unfortunately not many would be able to see the heaven sunrise. The God of *Love*, along with her sisters and brothers, pillaged the utopia, leaving nothing behind, with barely a trace of what magic was there. The seaside horse watched in depression at the sight of his home being burnt and torn apart. A few critters were able to make it to the shore, but it was only a pack of squirrels, two four-horned deer, and four fireflies. All their eyes watered like the sea viewing the atrocity caused by the God of *Love*. Quartz was helpless and really couldn't use her powers to escape her cage, but she did find herself a tool to break the wooden door.

With just her strength, she broke up the door and then quickly ran to aid the animals, but she was too late. She stood far away from her mother, watching what she once called a village slaughter the rest of the animals on the shore; they robbed them of their skins and cleaned the furs and bones by the sea, and the horse had drowned itself in the sea, not to be seen anymore. Quartz hoped for them not to die; her mother did not live up to her power. She yelled at the top of her lungs, begging for Death to come, till her wish came true. Just from above, a red light beamed on the shoreline. A fire blaze broke through the atmosphere, and eventually, a fireball landed in the sand. Yetzer had arrived to collect his bounty. After the smoke cleared and the evaporating water had been poured into the air, Yetzer rose from his landing and declared, "I've come to kill the Demigod Quartz. Stand in my way, and you will die too." With his blood eyes, he saw the demigod staring at him alone on top of the hill and charged, his hands with red energy. The townspeople were commanded by their queen to keep her daughter safe at all costs, but it was no use going against this firebender. One by one each villager came and tried their attacks on the volcanic demigod, but none of them survived.

They reached for an attack, but Yetzer blasted away his enemies with ash, disintegrating them from the Nimmer he held. He set fire to the flesh and threw away the bodies he grabbed by the neck, and Death had been carrying a sack on his back during the rampage. The God of *Love* had seen Death from afar while guarding her daughter with her arms. She called out to the antihero, pleading with him to stop the rageful slaughtering. Death couldn't do anything. After all, he had to obey the foundation. Quartz's life was up to her mother to protect, and so she went forward to combat Yetzer.

The last farmer-turned-soldier had fallen, leaving Yetzer and the God of *Love* at a standstill. Yetzer had intimidatingly said to the god before him, "Move. Or else you will die with the rest of your people." The God of *Love* stood her ground, waving her hands in a shape where she made an invisible light pink wall between herself and Yetzer. He had gotten closer, touching the wall and taking in the details of the lovely sparkles. It didn't hurt him once he touched it, so he set his hands to red energy, and with his right hand, he broke through the wall like glass, grabbing the throat of his obstacle.

In defense, the God of *Love* placed both of her hands on his forehead, and using her power, she tried to give him love but his mind and heart were filled with hate and anger, irreplaceable because of his father. Yetzer screamed as her powers were working but not for long. As a counter move, he ignited his entire body in his red glow that greatly damaged the hands he was being held by. He squeezed the throat of his opponent, and soon enough, he turned her flashes into a black cloud of ash. Disintegrating her skin to bones, he dropped the corpse on the sand and whispered, "Your love is weakness." The God of *Love* had become the first god to die. Her death had brought a knockback blast of rose petals, a ripple effect that stained the sand and ocean right where Yetzer had stood. The water was cursed with a light-pink hue around the edges of where it came on the sand, and a sparkling effect was left in the air where her last moments were. Royally, Death had collected the soul of the fallen friend from the sand and left it in fading smoke.

Yetzer had been stunned at the sudden arrival of his kill count. He had killed a god. Quartz had a source to pull from to acquire her full power, and just like Yetzer, she had become infuriated. Quartz spawned a blade of rose gold and proceeded to climb down to the shore. Standing a football field away, she, with anger, was ready to avenge her fallen mother. Up until now, she was not a fighter, but she was willing to do her best. Ready for another fight, Yetzer had ignited his hands and then rushed his way toward Quarts, but she hadn't moved and therefore suffered for hesitation. Yetzer, with flaming hands, threw a fireball at Quartz while he was still in motion. He was only halfway when he threw the fire at her, and Quartz tried to block this incoming attack but her sword was no use in cutting it into two. When the blaze had come into contact with her skin, it didn't do a lot of damage; but it did, however, cause her to fall backward and stumble. Yetzer had already been at her location with daggers in hands. Quartz had fortunately dodged all of Yetzer's attacks when she had come up to him, swinging his arms.

Quarts had returned attacks of her own, swinging as if she were Athena. Yetzer was a good fighter, and his Nimmer powers enhanced his combat ability. Eventually, Yetzer had enough of the games when both demigods were on the defensive with each other. They faced each other—red bloom beams from one's hands and fourteen flamingo-colored glass blades in the other's. These demigods called them weapon. Yetzer had used his finisher. His eyes and mouth glowed in cinnabar red, and his brimstone face peaked with energy. Beams of scarlet Nimmer came from his eyes and mouth. Quartz held her sword in blocking the force flames. She got pushed back inch by inch while holding on to her sword of light, trying her best to block, but it was no use. Her blade was shattered into dust, and her face was marked by the energized crimson. The blast had thrown her away across the beach. There she lay on her back, staring at the sky. Close to death, she breathed in her final moments when she knew she had been defeated. Yetzer came walking down to collect the second soul. He stood over her, engulfed in horror maroon.

He looked down at her, not with empathy. "Aren't you the demigod of *Love*?" He said. Quartz shook her head up and down as a tear fell from her cheek. He continued, "Then why are you so weak?" A grin took over Yetzer's lips as he completed his task of killing one of the seven demigods. Yetzer burrowed his red hands into Quartz's chest cavity, grabbing her heart and tearing it out. He crushed her crystal heart with his dark-red nova-powered hands and began to absorb her power to love. Death had spawned, soothing Quartz's agony. Yetzer couldn't see Death, but Quartz could see him.

"Hello, darling. Come with me. Someone is waiting for you," Death said to the demigod of *Love* respectfully. He held her hand, and both walked away into a light. Yetzer's arms glowed, morphing from light pink to his shade of blood. He had harnessed the power and grew stronger than before. He had new abilities he didn't have before. He now could fly, and his beams did more damage.

CHAPTER IV

COBALT BLUE VERSUS VOID RED

Yetzer's father had spawned on the sand just a shore away from him. "Your mission is not over till you bring me all those demigod powers." It was not a congratulatory message nor a sincere apology for the missed opportunity to speak about his feelings of success. Yetzer looked behind the sea to the sun. Behind the sun lay a faraway planet of oil stones. Yetzer had not only felt powerful but he also somehow felt a mix of energy, both unbalanced and balanced. He was tired, and now the sand seemed like a good resting place maybe for a minute or two.

"I am tired. Perhaps I'll rest for now." The God of *Power* found this as a weakness and would not allow excuses.

Just as Yetzer was about to lay down on the soft moisturizer sand, his father yanked him and continued with "No son of mine will rest till I feel satisfied. I will not allow you to rest until I feel as though you have earned it!" Perhaps it was here and these moments where anger fueled his power to be everlasting. Yetzer wanted to cry, but would that weaken his power of rage red? To be calm in sorrow blue, his father did not take such pity, for he expected the best at all times.

"Okay, Father, I won't rest." Standing side by side, bathing in rays from the star, Yetzer continued to play his father's game.

Meanwhile far away from this planet stayed the demigod of *Destruction*. His father found this planet in paradise, so he saw it fit to turn the land into new. What he had changed was that this planet was now gloriously full of doom, with ghost skies and rotting land. The God of *Destruction* rained fire and boomed the planes till rivers turned to oil and no trees stood, only skyscrapers of glass. It was the City of Pandemonium. He annihilated most of the creatures that had lived; they became a new species, from four-legged beasts to two-legged rock spirits. The Merikuh replaced the old and were the only ones who lived here. They did not come from Asherah, for these were new and didn't cause any problems from God herself.

In her mind, she created the universe. Wasn't that enough? "Why must I work more when I've already done more than enough?" she said then vanished, not being seen by any of the gods. Eventually, her actions of rest will have consequences. A long time from now, there will be a demigod who will challenge her rule, questioning her very existence, but for now, we focus our attention on Regin, the demigod of *Destruction*. He was made up of the same elements as his fellow brothers and sisters, the combined forces of half rock and ghost. Spirits that had rocks of obsidian in different spots and sizes formed all of the body. What made Regin different was not that he was a demigod but how his dark purple body glowed. Unlike the others with the same element, they didn't glow in the night like he did. He lived in a highly advanced world, with towers of colored glass.

Silver replaced metal, ash replaced rain, and hardly any trees or vegetation rooted in soil. Magic was the new technology; spawning food and things for living was the norm. Though certain Merikans could do these things, not everyone could develop magic. The God of *Destruction* created/spawned a general to command his army when he wasn't around. A sword stuck in brown grass with blood drawn was the method to cast such evil creatures.

Asmodée, the demonic creature of lust, the manipulative beast of those trapped sexual desires. He was spawned by the blue magic coming from the hands of his god, the destroyer. Asmodée stood tall in a field of cobblestone. He was the size of a mammoth while in front of his creator. "In all reasonable ways, me, here, and how?" the voice of sin said, rasping against hell stone, a distorted voice that could only have come from a place of firestorm symbolism.

The God of *Destruction* had returned his line while looking at the colossal being. "Be my commander. Cast the sexiest curse however you feel. Make my arms strong so you won't have to stay in the inferno any longer."

The demon laughed as if the joke was the god himself and not the request. "Who seeks my aid of desired doomed intimacy?"

The God of *destruction* had seemed tiny compared to the enormous seventh king of hell. To prove his worthiness in the presence of great malice, he said, "Summon your greatest warrior of limbo. If I defeat them, you serve me, but if they defeat me, I serve you." Asmodée, with a chuckle, flipped a large wooden coin engraved with gold on the ground, almost squishing the god. He turned his back to walk away and position himself in the viewpoint of the show.

Crawling out of the wood, dipped in maroon that faded ghostly, was the demon ZoZo, the elite employee of hell. He stood with rotting flesh, almost like a zombie. He had robes of souls, claws that were like a troll, a bloody face, and the power of soul-snatching. ZoZo screamed in a cat-like posture, and its mouth snapped off to enlarge itself. Suddenly a flock of ravens came swarming out, and they flew around the two competitors. The crows flew in the air, hawking down below. ZoZo said to its enemy, "Be laid to rest. Be done till the sun goes down. Just like my king, he will rise again. Die forever till I release you from my chains of test!"

The God of *Destruction* had formed two normal silver swords in each hand—nothing special, not holy, no powers, nor did they grant any extra abilities. Standing on guard against his opponent, ZoZo lunged at the god, reaching out with its hands ready to grab his throat. The god swung at the neck of the demon while at the same time sliding under. It was clean and slick; off came the head. Oil of malice spread and stained the ground, which rotted where the body had landed. The final growls came from the beast, its last word. The crows, as a last stand, came down, their beaks sharp as the sun. In combating the airborne enemies, the God of *Destruction* had thrown an infinite amount of daggers one by one at the birds, striking in the eyes and wings. There were twelve of them that were laid to rest in a crown shape. The birds lay just above their dead demon. Speaking of the dead, Death had risen from each corpse and then collectively fell into the sky into nothingness. Asmodée gasped, for now, he was the servant to someone. "Promise kept you alive, now must be I." The silver blades had vanished in blue smoke, and Asmodée honored the god. They walked back to the designated city in which the seventh demon king was appointed the ruler over the army. Reign had become friends with the demon, his only friend. Though Asmodée did bad, still Reign looked past it.

Meanwhile, Yetzer left the planet to continue his mission. He could survive in deep space because the Nimmer kept him from the cold and lack of oxygen. It took Yetzer about a full seven days before he ever got to the planet home of the demigod. He admired the colors in such a void place. From the stars to the worlds, all of them seemed to touch Yetzer and his cold heart. It made him think. "Do I act for myself?" It sent a haunt down his back; he was beginning to learn more of what it meant to be a free thinker. But one contradiction was not about to stop him from following orders. Moreover, in the City of Pandemonium, there had been an attack on the capital by its citizens. The God of *Destruction* was absent from the people's lives for the most part; that meant Asmodée was the prime leader. He didn't care for the people, and they all knew it. They could tell he was more evil than their god. There was a symbolic color change of leadership. There was cobalt blue on flags, on the many rocks in the streets, and on the weapons the soldiers held. Now with Asmodée as the head of all, it all had changed from blue to the nasty brown slug color of lust. He didn't do anything evil to a larger extent; though on his first day as general, he had done the unexpected.

On the seventh afternoon, when the soldiers had finished working out for the day, they had all gone to the showers as a traditional group activity. Asmodée had caught the smell of the men. Though the demon was in its home chamber, that didn't stop his power from reaching the soaked men. He telepathically poisoned the men's minds; he planted the idea to have a sin party. He, the lust king, commanded the men to have their way with each other. Asmodée didn't care if they were men. He wanted to see the aftermath's destructive results. The moans of pleasure echoed across the base, and the showers had become a heated abyss.

NIMMER

It was all created by the lust king himself. The citizens were in a riot, and the demigod had been MIA. All of these actions would lead to the fall of this empire. The God of *Destruction* had stayed in the crystal city, for he would try to bring the gods together for dinner. Even if he was walking mass destruction, he had a heart, and he used it many times. Kindness came at a cost. He stayed out of his city for too long and when all seemed right in his head. His crown would be knocked down. Night fell, and the low magenta and watercolor cadmium yellow glowed under the stars. The city was asleep but not for long, for it had been seven days. Yetzer had been on his way, ready, and didn't hesitate to kill the first person he saw. Upon entering the planet, he had a feeling that the city was where the demigod stayed. What also led him that way was the loud uproar of the city hall. The blue fire held in the air and it drew Yetzer closer to grasp more. He slowly began to float down to the rioters then asked one with the standard, "I am looking for the demigod that rules here. Would you mind telling me where he is?"

ROMEO VEGA

The rock citizen had pushed away the magma demigod in rudeness. He stated, "Buzz off, brimstone boy." Yetzer let the anger go because he was already on a mission and didn't bother getting sidetracked. He flew away to the top of the building they had been positioned in front of. He figured that the people might be mad at him, and this is where he lay. Using his red hands to blast a hole while hanging in the air, he floated down to the base floor of a dark room. Sculptures in glass cages lined up in rows, in many sizes and materials, ranging from bronze to quartz.

Down the hall was a door, a gold-engraved wooden door, with Asmodeé's signature sigil in the middle. This corrupted, crooked hall was the entrance to hell that Yetzer was walking down. He feared nothing and no one for that matter. The dark matter cursed the floor and walls, peeling the paint and taking the pure color out. Yetzer readied his power for a fight, igniting the flame storm within his hands. Across the door stood the demon, with his oil-brown gunk reptilian skin. An arena for a room, Asmodeé chuckled while a slope of trash fell from his mouth. He was viewing the minds of the men while they had gathered after the showers, where they had now been arguing about their mentality, and at first, he didn't see Yetzer standing. So at this moment, Yetzer took account of the environment.

The repulsive demon was theoretically lying on a pile of trash, but his figure was so massive that his feet, legs, and knees were all tucked in his belly. The obese brute stopped looking into the minds, taking notice of the sandman that stood before him. "Are you another god who wishes to bargain with me?"

Yetzer stood front and center then replied, "I am no god asking for a trade. I am looking for the demigod who rules this planet. Do you know where he stands?"

Asmodeé laughed. "The best of friends, we are. What is your business with him?"

Yetzer levitated and flew closer and closer to the demon; the demigod was tired of the firewall that stood before him. "I am not a man of patience. Bring him to me, for I will bring death to your eyes and have you laugh in an ache." The two had a stare down, but Asmodeé broke the tension with a loud chuckle.

He continued, "Many men with power come to me for a bargain. Overpower me and you will be given your answer to the question by my corpse connecting to your mind." Yetzer accepted this challenge. His face turned into a volcano where cracks of lava ran down his eyelids, and the eyes themselves beamed off River Phoenix. He became the death-filled burning light. Asmodeé had spawned an army of black ghostly creatures—you could say that they were demons but not quite.

Yetzer had landed on the ground, looking around and observing the circle he was in. The minions had their prey surrounded. Four from the crowd ran toward Yetzer, but he was ready. Yetzer balled his fist and then aimed at the head of what was running. His arm had become a rifle; a beam of red came from his fist, killing the enemy. One by one they fell as he aimed and fired at the heads. He turned in circles with his arms moving and shifting in different directions. He had an unusual fighting style; it was reckless, but in a way, it was as if he were liquid. He appeared as lava, and he moved as such.

Such rage he held in his mind and stone heart while in battle. As each black soul fell, he gained strength, he could carry on fighting because it was an infinite push-and-pull system. It was like the saying "As I take life, so as I gain life." Asmodeé stopped the battle between the inferno and his ghost. "You flame of death creature! Spill your mind in the announcement of your source of power!" The lust king had enough of being powerless. He thought, *Who better than to take such power away?* He called forth Yetzer, but once more, the demigod, as well, had enough of the games.

"For an entity your size, I'd expect a larger power." As a final blow, Yetzer had opened his face, revealing a weapon, the same power he used to kill the last demigod. He blasted a supervolcano at his enemy. With the melting of the reptile skull and bones, Asmodeé screamed in agony, and after the brutal slaughter, he perished with fire and ash landing on his many possessions of sex symbols. His corpse fell, but what rose from his body were two things: the answer, and Death. Of course, Death came first. The same black ball of life came out of the body and flew into the sky for it to disappear. Next out came a light of whispers from the fallen demon's brain. The light inched closer and closer to Yetzer for it to be absorbed into his skin.

The eyes widened, for he had seen where the demigod stayed. Yetzer saw his enemy meditating in a hue of blue and black. Reign had been alone in a flat field, learning how to use his powers of mass destruction. Yetzer, now leaving the colosseum of hell, flew back out to find his way to kill the demigod of *Destruction*. While Yetzer set his destination, Reign was on the other side of the planet, which hadn't been so corrupted. A blue mist/hue came from the black stone that lay just a few feet behind Reign. Where Reign stood was on grass, but behind him was what seemed to be the ending of a volcanic eruption. The stone gave off a steam of blue. It wasn't poisonous to the demigods; it did, however, slightly enhance Reign's powers. He felt it in his joints. He was able to explode to the ground using his mind, kind of like his father, but Reign could only do it to a small extent of land. With his father, he could explode the ground that was the size of an entire county; Reign could only explode the size of a twenty-eight-story building. He was destructible.

Reign had adopted a unique fighting style, a style that consisted of stealth and swift attacks. It was similar to a ninja but more powerful in its ability to attack. What these gods were using was a different type of magic rather than the basic illusion. This type of magic was a religious and cosmic power. When Reign exploded the ground, there weren't particles of light. The same went for all the gods whenever they used their powers. The demigod of *Destruction* used smoke as his ally. Whenever he exploded the group, a dirt cloud spread throughout the area. He, however, could see well enough through the clouds, and here he looked for points of attack. He had practiced this technique while Yetzer was on his way. Both teams had prepared, but Reign hadn't known he had a bounty on his head. Either way, he was ready for his opponent.

Hiding in the dust, adopted by the stealth, were both self-taught demigods. After a while, Yetzer reached his destination. Reign could see the void red killer from the sky. He resembled a death light, the dying carmine-red creature. Reign felt his death near, just by the sight of the falling ash that swarmed the battlefield. Yetzer stayed in the sky when gazing at the demigod of *Destruction*, but Reign had no desire for an eye contest. "You there. Of which origins do you come from?"

Yetzer slowly descended to the ground just a foot away from the demigod. "Nimmer. A planet away from here." Igniting his hands in red flames, Reign took notice and pulled blades of blue from his lower back while also preparing his ground moves by digging his foot in the dirt.

"What is it that has you here, away from home?"

Yetzer, with a grin, said, "You." Yetzer had walked closer, but not to cause a fight so soon; Reign had asked more from his enemy.

"And who's the name of your leader that you follow?"

In conflict with himself, Yetzer said, "My father?" In this vulnerable position, Reign had tried to use this to his advantage. There are many stages a fight can have, ranging from a mental battle to a physical fight.

NIMMER

"Do you have a mind of your own to think for yourself?" It was a troubling question for the fire demigod, for he had never thought of such actions. And probably this was where his most of his characteristics came into play.

"Do I have to listen?" Yetzer pleaded.

The wise words came from his unsure enemy, "No. You have a mind. Use it wisely. No such creature should have their mind in a cage, most of all you." The God of *Power* could hear his plan falling apart.

He could feel his son's heartstrings being pulled. So he whispered in his son's mind, "Kill him. He is trying to stop you from gaining power. No son of mine will have a heart." So Yetzer, with deep lies in his head, pulled power from his anger and engulfed himself in red. With a scream of rage, he threw a wave of red energy at his enemy with a swing of his whole arm. The damage came from the fingertips down to his elbow. Once he let go of the energy, it flew out of his hands. Reign blocked this attack with his swords of midnight blue, creating an electric light of purple around the blades themselves. The demigod, with no other choice, blew up the ground, casting smoke and ensuing the battle between the two polar opposite colors. This was Reign's time to shine and use what he had practiced. He not only blew up the green ground but also the blue volcanic ground. So now, therefore, his blue blades blended in with the smoke that had covered the field. This was a cinematic scene of the void red standing in blue bust, casting a hue of purple. Yetzer had never fought in these circumstances, where his vision would be of no use to him, but this allowed him to use the mind rather than his hands.

Reign, on the other hand, had hidden in the dust. He would look at the bright-red hands and watch where they would attack. Then quickly and quietly, he stabbed Yetzer's legs with daggers of lapis and then disappeared without being seen. Reign had a plan to first take away the vision then the foundation and next the weapons themselves. The death red on Yetzer's hands never went away, even if all was against him. He never showed weakness to his enemies. As a counter move, Yetzer had let out a huge burst of red energy with the action of throwing his hands into the air. It somewhat cleared the blue smoke, but most importantly, it hit Reign in the chest. He was launched out of the blue dust bubble where Yetzer had a clear sight in the blue. And he walked out of the blue with bright-red hands. Reign had risen from the ground, harmed by his blades. Aggressively Yetzer threw waves of red energy at his opponent with Reign blocking these incoming shots with his blades. Each wave seemed stronger than the last. The blue blades had lost their color after the last blast, and even then Yetzer had come face-to-face with the demigod of *Destruction*, grabbing him by the throat and saying, "Tell me. Do you have a mind of your own?"

Of course, there was no response to the question because Reign knew the meaning behind that question. He had struggled in his position, but he found that cutting off the hand of his enemy worked in setting himself free. A loud pain cry came from the fire demigod. It came out to be black blood, but Yetzer had to act quickly because Reign was running toward the blue dust to hide once more. So with his other hand, Yetzer spawned a fireball of blood moon red. As Reign was about to enter, Yetzer struck him in the back then fell on the ground face first, just inches away from his blue safe haven. Close to defeat, the demigod crawled his way toward the dust, hoping to use this to his advantage. In the end, it was to no use. Reign couldn't blow anything up, and he couldn't create any new weapons. He was far too weak to use anything.

Yetzer had his companion, Death, by his side. Walking on grass but turning it into ash, he finally got to Reign and flipped him over, facing the sky. The two locked eyes, and for a second, they both seemed to find themselves in that same position. It was an emotional moment for the two gods—one of them controlled and the other free. Had the question about each other been asked first, things would have gone differently. "You put up a good fight, friend. Now I must go on a journey of death. Perhaps I'll see you in a different form of light." Those were the last words from the demigod of *Destruction*. The final blow came from Yetzer in the form of a powerful stomp to his opponent's face. Green and blue mucus came running out of the gore site. Death had spawned, standing at the feet of the soul he had to take.

CHAPTER V

Dark Nepeta Green versus Eternal Maroon Oak

Death had gazed upon the caged fire demigod, taking in the beast that could be so heartless. After a while, Death took the soul of the demigod and carried him to his father at the dinner table, which had been going on for some time. There an uproar from the father came. "Death, explain yourself for such an act to have my son by your side!" Such a statement caused much tension among the gods. Asherah told her fellow god to calm down.

"Death, do you have an announcement to clear?" God asked.

He said what every god feared most. "I believe calamity has arrived in the universe."

Reign ran to his father, and here they had welcomed each other in hugs. A wave of gasps came from the table, which were comprised of the God of *Destruction*, the God of *Universal Travel*, the God of *Power*, the God of *Worlds*, and finally the God of *Stars*.

A question came from the God of *Stars*. "This calamity isn't more powerful than you, correct?"

Death sent a laugh into the room. "I am Death. No living creature can conquer me." This assured all of them, but they noticed that two of their fellow gods hadn't shown up.

The God of *Worlds* asked the question, "This calamity couldn't perhaps be a god killer, could it?"

This was answered by Death and his unforgettable words. "Yes. You are missing your fellow gods for a reason." Here it hit their mind that this calamity was a god killer. A variety of emotions came from the table. A small panic came from the God of *Worlds*, but a calmness had been presented by the God of *Stars*.

NIMMER

A bargain came from the God of *Destruction*. "What can we do about this, Asherah!" It seemed as if they looked to her for all the answers, but all she could do was tell them to obey the foundation.

"So as you wish to do something with any action. However, avoid any to break our foundation." It was not a clear answer the gods wanted; however, the God of *Stars* had an idea to prepare his daughter for calamity if he couldn't intervene in a way where it broker the foundation. He had left the rest to fight for an answer.

Next to gain more knowledge, the God of *Worlds* asked an unthought question. "Have you any idea of where this calamity came from?"

Death stared down the God of *Power*, for he knew but to not cause any more damage to the Crystal City, he had said, "I simply know that it came from a planet called Nimmer, and this planet holds great power within its sand."

Confusion came from the God of *Worlds*, for he hadn't remembered to create such a planet with so much power. "I have no recollection of creating such a planet."

Death continued to look at the God of *Power*, but he chose to not speak of his actions. Instead he said with a goodbye, "Carry on. I have business to tend to if such calamity continues on."

Asherah said to the God of *Worlds* in the closing statement, "If I were you. I'd do the same to prepare your child for this eternal Nimmer." When he left, it was just Death who stood at the very end of the table and God who stood at the opposite end. God responded first, "Is there anything else you have to give, even if such things are impossible?"

The black ghost created such tension with his return statement. "Don't think for a second you can conquer me. I know where your power lies, and to tell you the truth, it's weak."

God hated being upstaged. "Death, you couldn't possibly be challenging your creator. Me of all beings in this universe."

Wandering/walking to the edge of the table while sliding his finger, he got ever closer to God. "I may hold the darkness, but don't mistake me for not carrying light as well," Death had said.

And once God spoke, each deity was face to face. "I knew you were going to be a problem in my universe," God said, then suddenly, she pulled a blade of white and stabbed Death in the stomach. Death himself seemed immune to God's unpredictable pain. He had flown her into that air and then thrown his creator's body on the table, shattering it in half.

Taking out the blade from his body with no complaint, he slowly descended upon his god and replied, "Every time I take a soul, almost every time, they think it is you they see." God lay defeated by Death, not responding. Then Death continued. "Here I see you sitting on this white throne doing nothing, not visiting your beloved creatures who wish to be seen only by you. I never bring them to you because you are a lazy god. I've created a dome for the souls I take. They seem happy, but you wouldn't know." In disgusted silence, Death disappeared without a trace, leaving God by herself in her own mess of tragedy.

Meanwhile, Yetzer stood at the sight of his victory. And he grew stronger once more; when his foot rose from the mind of the demigod, a surge of power rushed through his body. He grew to be more masculine than before and far more devilish in the form of two horns, not only did such a thing happen but it also healed his arm. In reptilelike fashion, it came back from the bone and then skin was the last thing. His father had appeared from the sky with information. "Dear boy. Death has found who you are. He could mess up my whole plan if he continues to have such an idea." Yetzer had aspirations for his newly acquired gear, but his father had no interest in his horns. "Listen, you fool! You must hurry and kill the rest of the demigods. I fear most of whom you have left are preparing for your arrival." Yetzer didn't like being called names, and though this was his second time, he still didn't like it. When his father said the word *fool*, Yetzer held the anger in and listened.

The God of *Destruction* had telepathically given Yetzer information of where the demigod Lawrence was. The demigod had his father come to him with fear in his eyes. The God of *Worlds* had never seen himself being a teacher of combat; though even before calamity, he never wanted his son to meet Death. You could say this calamity fueled him more to teach his son what powers he was capable of. "Don't mistake your own hands to just be skin and bone. Your hands carry so much power, for your real strength is how you use it," he once said on a day of celebration.

Back on the planet where Yetzer and his father had stood to talk, the God of *Destruction* had gone back home to his ravaged and torn city. The City of Pandemonium had suffered great consequences. First, it was a riot, then a civil war, then an outcome of carnage. A lot had died, but there were some civilians who remained either in the city or went off to form and find something new. Pandemonium looked completely different; the color was gone to wear, and it looked abandoned. Brown flags had washed the streets, and on cobblestone, bodies lay lifeless. It was an abandoned city.

The God of *Destruction* walked around, taking a gaze at his now-lost city, and eventually, he went into the town hall to find his army general, Asmodeé, lifeless. He didn't care for his dead demon assistant. He walked back outside to gain a rush of sadness, for he was alone in a broken city. He sat on the steps of the town hall, and here he wouldn't move until Death had come to collect him. While morning came to the god's face (one of many he would experience) and night fell upon the father and son, Yetzer left like a rocket, but while blasting off, the God of *Destruction* had seen and heard him fly away. In an unexpected twist, the God of *Power* had stayed to take in the beautiful view of the morning's blue volcanic ground. It was just enough time for his soon-to-be enemy to advance his way, and when his journey was completed by the two gods locking eyes, the God of *Destruction* demanded, "What are you doing here!"

The ground rumbled at the very voice, a manipulation tactic the God of *Destruction* used. "Don't believe your thoughts, dear brother. I'm only here to take a look at your darling planet." This did not work.

A crying scream came from the mouth of the grieving god. "You are the creator of this calamity, you!"

A laugh came from the red flag god. "Stand in my way, and you will see your son just as this light rises." With the eyes of a killer, he had no sympathy. His purpose had gotten the better of him, to be the symbol for all energy in the universe, but he took that job and craved to conquer.

"Ask Death to come. I am no god without reason to do my actions." It was such a lesson, that even gods can gain depression. So to a loose end, the God of *Power* had thrown red blades into the body of his fallen brother, who slowly died in the process. Then he quickly disappeared because he didn't want Death to see him once more. And of course, Death had arrived. The god wept on Death's shoulders and begged to be sent to his son, and Death did just that, reuniting the two deceased gods in the dome of Death.

In a solar system of eight planets stayed the God of *Worlds* and his offspring. They both had thoughts that there was something special about these many eight planets and the stories they held. For Lawrence, and in both of their minds, they were the last line of defense. This was their endgame, and for some reason, the idea of Death coming for them brought them together. These moments were the preferred father-son bonding time. They trained, they fought, and they grew strong. It should be noted that Lawrence was the Prince Charming of his little village. He was a handsome young fella; not only did he look the part to be a classical hero, but also his father made sure his battle reflected that. He found a way to use the oils and minerals to achieve such soft and clean skin by taking out the very essence of the world and pairing it with his own layer of self. He had a passion for discovery—an attractive trait, it seemed, for some of the women in the village. Though Lawrence's father suggested otherwise that he have relationships, considering he was made to be a soldier. It was a similar parallel to his future enemy.

Speaking of him, he had been in deep space again on his way to continue this calamity. Though in flight, he had a conversation with himself about what Reign had said to him about being a free thinker. "Do I have a free mind?" he contemplated. Not getting emotional, he didn't know if his father was in his head or was always watching. Nevertheless, he was coming. Lawrence had nearly become a planet bender (his home planet was not Earth, so therefore any planet he visited, he could use the surface for his gain). With his knowledge of how to move the planet by the teachings of his father, he positioned his hands in ways to form rocks. Each direction he moved his hands in meant something new. On a day of sunrise, the God of *Worlds* had asked his son to join him in hunting. Once they got to a forest of watercolor yellow, they sat on a bird to eat for dinner. It had been perfectly perched in view.

The God of *Worlds* told his son to pull back his arm as if he were shooting a bow and arrow, but with this type of archery, the "arrow" was a sharp object of rock or wood formed from the ground beneath. Lawrence didn't feel right killing an innocent bird, but his father had brought up a point. "Death comes to all. Never mistake him to be an enemy." As gods themselves, Lawrence couldn't think of what to give to balance this world. The ask to take; the permission to give. With the pullback of his arm and the release of both his breath and arm, Lawrence had taken a life, and with this life, he would give life to his family to eat. It was a simple balance he had to comprehend.

The demigod had a color with him. The wisdom was green, being able to see life and death as one. His primary choice to wear green was to have rings of nepeta. On his home planet, he went to a cave behind a black waterfall, and here he found stones of green. He picked up five of them and carved them using his powers, using his fingers to drill into them, making them more and more a ringlike shape. He put three on his right hand and two on his left. The rings didn't make his power any better or worse, but he believed it when he would practice with his father. Wherever he walked, his green traveled; he was the wise wiz the village had cherished. It took about one full year and one day for Yetzer to finally reach his bounty. In the meantime, Lawrence had some stories to tell—many of which were about him and his father but also about gathering a group of friends, the local outlaws. They were a group even before Lawrence tagged alongside. They were somewhat bounty hunters across the universe.

However, they didn't just hunt wanted people. For example, if someone/a customer went up to one of them asking for an object or protection, for the right price, they would be up for the job. Sometimes Lawrence didn't see eye to eye with their morals. The brawler of the ground had no problem sending any being to Death, and this upset Lawrence. He knew Death wasn't the enemy, but to him, that didn't mean sending creatures to him for no reason. For example, on a faraway planet, there had been a raid, and of course, the bandits had brought Lawrence with them to help. They particularly had him because they knew what he could do. They had all traveled via an ornamental root. This root could spawn a portal to travel to wherever the holder of the plant wanted to go. It is said that this plant the root grew on the planet where the God of *Universal Travel* had bled during a battle between her and an enemy.

Supposedly, her blood landed on the ground, and the roots soaked in her power. The plant had glowed and gained an aura of phoenix gold. This plant eventually attracted the bounty hunters in their early years. The leader, symbolized by the red bandanna he wore on his face, sought it for only him to use such power, and to use this plant, someone would just hold it and think of the location. But it had to be a place where the holder had been before. They all had been to the planet they were traveling to with the raid in place before, and with Lawrence by their side, they had a fighting chance, because the last time they were there, it had ended with retreating to safety along with fallen blood.

The leader of the party had stood in front and spawned the portal. To Lawrence's knowledge, he was breaking chains off from the village—an act of kindness, that's all he knew and was told. He was never told that the bandits were the cause of the raid. Then just as they all united the portal to a sight of flame, the leader charged forward into battle as if he were the symbol for the legendary fearmonger. The rest had followed behind, but Lawrence had hesitated in this action. He was told by body language that what he had to do just didn't seem right. His friends had adventured into war presumably ready to die for one another. The more he looked and took in the chaos, the more he realized he was the enemy. He knew even then that if he hadn't started the flames nor had been within the area, he still traveled and walked among his fellow friends and chose to uphold their actions.

They had fought as one in the dry and dead cornfield. Lawrence had looked around and saw multiple people (notably children) alone either in their houses or lying on the ground after an injury. While the bandits had been in different parts of the village taking apart the limbs (the only way to make sure they were really dead) of the men and women who lived in the bellhouses, Lawrence had recused some children by shifting the land to one far away from the village, or like one instance where a child was trapped in a burning house, from right outside, Lawrence used the floor to make a cocoon, sheltering the child from the fire till it was completely gone. Just then, as the rebels came to find Lawrence with a child behind his legs. He and the leader had a stare down. The leader, with an eye for revenge, said, "You think these children you saved have a god?!" No word back from the demigod. "Our god has abandoned us, Lawrence! Why should they be given the right!" A mighty voice had shaken the souls in the radius.

"I have no knowledge of who they are. What I do know is that killing them is not right. I'm sorry for whatever happened in your life, but spreading carnage is not what a leader in red should uphold." Still, in defense of the child, that speech wasn't meant for encouragement nor inspiration. Lawrence had used his fearful heart as either a weapon or a shield. The traitor had given Lawrence the chance to finally be with the team or not. He either established their friendship and followed their code or died doing what is right, which meant leaving these people. Lawrence said with such a rebellious attitude, "I will never be led by your twisted logic of killing for revenge. Maybe in another life where your god hadn't left, we'll meet again and be better." No argument came from the leader. With that closing statement, the group all traveled in a portal, leaving Lawrence alone with the children.

The people in question were scarecrows, walking hay bales with arms and legs. They didn't have any fingers or toes. The ends of the tips were straw, and their face had indents of a face. Their "flesh" was made of hay, and they wore brown pants and shirts, though it should be noted that when they all came to Lawrence, everyone (the male and female) had an attractive aura to him—perhaps this was about his good looks or the honor he waved around. It is unknown how they operated as a society, by any man-made ideology such as communism or capitalism. They seemed like nice beings and hardworking individuals without the constructive consequences of human beliefs.

Lawrence had saved about eighteen people on that day of ruination, though he wished he could have done more. One by one they all came from different parts of the village. There were some adults with no children of their own anymore, but they still shook the demigod's hand. And all the kids came to his legs and started clinging to them. Eventually, a crowd of 167 people began to gather all around him and kneel. Of course, the children sat crisscrossed. They all had looked up to him as God; he didn't want to be, but he didn't want to take away hope so quickly. He could see that the kids were fairly starved, so as a gift, he had grown with his powers some different colored pink and yellow fruits that had grown on bright-green bushes. A few feet away came running children, and within seconds, all eighteen of them had stuffed their faces on the fruits that had grown in health.

As the children sat and ate as a group a few steps away from their parents, Lawrence had all the parents huddled around him, sitting or kneeling. Lawrence wanted to know more about what had happened, so he asked one injured father. "What caused this to happen to you all?" The father wept in silence. It was perhaps because he had lost his daughter or himself; either way, he had no response for the demigod. And so he asked once more, but this time a pregnant woman.

"There is a word of a god killer. He comes to any planet and takes the lives of gods. That is why this has happened. They've gone insane without their god." Stumbling on her words, she wept in such fear. She hadn't seen this figure she spoke of, but her knowledge of the stories were far too sinister and known. Lawrence was deeply worried not only for his safety but for his father's too.

He had asked one more final question, which was, How long ago was it when the last god was killed? "A full rotation ago!" cried someone in the back, anonymously. Lawrence had stood up with determination and anger. He had the ability to fly and survive in space. He had taken a small part of the planet (a variety of metals) and formed a gadget that would make him able to breathe. As he flew high in the sky, looking underneath his feet, he had spawned more of the growing bushes to keep feeding the children; and the partners began to reach for the skyline, worshiping this entity that had cared for them. Lawrence had rushed back to his planet, in determination to put an end to this god killer, which it was of course Yetzer they had been talking about. The term *god killer* had probably been created simply by the theory that there had been a survivor on the same planet where the God of *Love* had been killed and they had left because of the sight of her death. Soon that story had spread throughout the universe.

Both demigods had been in space, reaching for the prize of a champion. For Lawrence, knowing his father had still been alive was his reward, and for Yetzer, killing one more demigod was his trophy. Eventually, Lawrence had reached his home. Word of mouth had said that his father was at the edge of the village on a hill, looking at the sky. So walking up the said hill during dusk, he had asked a question from a distance. It was known that the God of *Worlds* would spend long periods of time meditating, but this time, he wasn't; he was simply taking in the sky and land, his own creation. And out of respect, Lawrence had always done this type of behavior. "Father?" the child asked, to which an answer of grim had responded.

"I believe you are ready for your final trial. I want you to know that when Death comes to you, know that I was never disappointed in you. The wise know when to listen, and I have heard calamity calling."

With no hesitation, Lawrence ran to his father with a hug of love and appreciation. "I will try my best in completing this trail." Both gods had quietly wept, and here it seemed to be an icebreaker moment.

"Did you live a life worth having?" With that question, the sun fell and the universe showed itself. Lawrence answered the many questions his father had about the journeys he came across. Sooner or later, with the passing of time, the God of *Worlds* put on a puppet show on the ground made up of dirt and rock. He was the best storyteller, with such drama and laughter. The burning light rose once more. Yetzer had arrived in the atmosphere with a roar of his lava skin breaking the sky. This signal was the God of *World's* first line of defense; knowing when your enemy has arrived is an upper hand itself. The gods woke from their slumber and set their eyes upon the red-oak demigod.

The God of *Worlds*, wearing a rubbish dark-moss robe stood and created a mountain as the arena of battle. Yetzer flew down on the mountaintop, and the gods had traveled to him via a lane of stars leading to the top. As they walked, Lawrence had crafted an iron chest plate, and arm guards equipped with little emerald stones, the same as his rings. He looked like a metal iguana. He was not a knight but a champion of wisdom, which fueled him with determination and anger. Perhaps here he was losing the point of trial and error. His father quickly noticed this emotion because he was here once too. He said to him, "Remove your anger. If you let your emotions get the better of your hard work, you will eventually lack discipline." Lawrence took a deep breath and calmed himself down and had his heart charge his power rather than his anger.

Yetzer stood in the dawn's light. Where his robe flared up in the wind, the villain was symbolized as the hero. Corrupted whispers came from the demigod's father over the shoulder. "Don't let them see you bleed." It was the final statement before sending his child into war against the gods.

Speaking of which, they both had come up from the stairs to meet Yetzer. "Are you preferred by a name?" asked the god of *Worlds*.

An uncomfortable silence was caused by the flamed demigod, but soon enough he spoke in the tone of a hellish snake. He looked like the devil, and he spoke like the demon king. "Yetzer," he said.

"You will challenge me first, then my son," the father said while also stepping at an angle in front of Lawrence.

"In flames, you will feel my rage. This world will die along with you and your child," Yetzer finally said, then his hands glowed in red but he was not doing anything more except getting himself into position for the fight.

Lawrence stood still as a tree, calm and ever silent, walking to the bottom of the stairs and leaving his father behind. The God of *Worlds* had committed to his fight attack against his opponent, which was a series of obsidian spikes that came from the mountain and rose from behind him. There were twelve in total, all launched at very fast miles per hour. Though these spikes were somewhat useless, Yetzer had blocked all of them with his four arms by crossing them in an x form. He had been wounded on the face, the oil of Nimmer oozing out from under his eye and his four arms too. Such a scare he earned, but as he broke his father's request, he in turn had suddenly become furious. The horns had set aflame then. He rose from the ground and had fired out several fireballs while attempting to swirl around the mountain to make himself harder to become a target.

The God of *Worlds* had protected himself with rocks made up from the mountain. He eventually found himself in a cocoon of stone; the amount of walls he had protected himself with had trapped him. Though being the creator of worlds, he could also break his world. So as a counter move, he had burrowed into the mountain and rose from another place along the side; a trident of emerald rose along with its creator. All the while, Yetzer was in the air, looking for his opponent and slowly destroying the illusion egg with some blasts in several types of ways.

ROMEO VEGA

Then suddenly the trident had stabbed Yetzer in the arm, which had caused him to fall. The grace of his fall had him symbolically show the world that no such creature could replace him. It was the irony of the fallen angel.

The battle had moved to the ground, just on the edge of where the mountain was. In a twist of delinquent behavior, Lawrence had taken the sight of the fallen god lying down motionless; he sprinted off to make sure he had no more fuel to burn. Just as Lawrence had gotten close to the flame, it became alive once more, and in an old fashion, Yetzer grabbed Lawrence's throat. But he was fairly trained, so he had created boulders to hold Yetzer's legs. Then Lawrence had pulled out the trident, which had released him, for the death grab. Yetzer had finally met an opponent that put up worthy fights. He cried in anger when an unusual amount of his black blood had come pouring out from his arm. With Lawrence's creative thinking, he had Yetzer trapped, and the two gods stared into each other's eyes—the limbo eyes of fire and the jungle green eyes.

Lawrence had said his frosty sentence to the calamity. "Your reign shall end here."

NIMMER

Yetzer hadn't noticed the intimidating attitude, but to match the same energy, Yetzer had delivered his response. "You see these horns? They are from your fallen friends." Suddenly a rush of punches passed Yetzer's face, brutal blows to both the face and hips. He not only used his fist, but at one point, he had also formed knuckle spikes in a metallic metal. For a second, he looked like an X-Men of some kind, Lawrence had such power that he broke Yetzer out of his caged legs. Then just in time, his father dug himself out of the ground. Now the demigod was standing in front, and his father was standing behind Yetzer. He was cornered, but he wasn't going to let that get the better of him. Suddenly both at once the demigod and his father rushed for Yetzer, with several attacks from both directions. The ground had moved to Yetzer's disadvantage, but he was able to dodge these obstacles of rock.

Both these gods had tried their hardest to defeat this walking Nimmer. Unfortunately, the God of *Worlds* had been overpowered. Yetzer had flown back to the top of the mountain, carried by the feet, and then he brutally slammed his enemy on the ground on his back. Something appeared to be broken. Lawrence, however, in a shameful act, had been knocked unconscious during their fight at the bottom of the stairs. When he came to, he rushed to his father's aid. In his last breath, the God of *Worlds* said, "The creation of your world was an accident, dear boy."

Yetzer stood over the God of *Worlds* with a response worthy of evil. "Power isn't an accident if it holds a purpose." Just as he said that, suddenly in supersized moments, Lawrence had risen, and the demigods locked eyes.

Lawrence had said with brutality, "I will rip and tear the very Nimmer from brittle bones." And here an aura of dark green shined from the stones on the armor. At this moment in time, not a single god knew that anger was the key to power. Such strong emotions seemed to unlock a great potential for the demigods.

Yetzer had used the two daggers by his side to throw, but ultimately, they were unable to break the skin of Lawrence. And he, too, had rolled on the floor, kneeling next to his fallen father; and he created a shield of cobblestone to protect the both of them from the swings of Yetzer's scarlet blades. Though this shield was not designed to withstand such Nimmer, so with one final plan from the world's gods, the god of *Worlds* had the idea to create a blue stone that was merely the very source of power itself. Lawrence, all the while, had started creating a staff to hold the stone in place, but suddenly, Yetzer's red energy broke down the shield and hit the stone. And here with both gods powers combined, the stone absorbed the Nimmer and the pure strength of the God of *Worlds*. It was two versus one for the stone. Yetzer had no knowledge of the purpose of the stone, but he could tell the God of *Worlds* was dying due to the collision of all three gods focusing their power on this one stone.

Eventually, once Yetzer had been exhausted from giving his all to the stone, he backed up to the edge of the mountain, kneeling in a restful manner. Once the blend of colors started to disappear, Lawrence had gone to his father absent from his own life, with the blue-stones staff lying next to him in a glowing yawn. Death had stood over Lawrence, placing his hand on his shoulder then taking his father's soul with them both exiting. In such pain Lawrence had been; he had a parallel to his enemy. He must have been so wise to turn this anger into cautiousness. "I am my enemy if I repeat my actions as them. I am no hero if I am one and the same as my fallen brother." He lived to this day, and he had forgotten about his number one rule.

These gods have so many layers to them, having the ability to create and destroy things from their very hands, but they have emotions. So in turn that makes them dangerous, but the wisest of the demigods realize that they mustn't be like the enemy. True power is how one handles the privilege of such great capability. "You feel that, the suffering? That's where me and you are alike." Yetzer said in an antitaging manner. The stone itself had been left alone by Yetzer till the day when it would be picked up once more.

"I am nothing like you," Lawrence claimed, now rising from his father's corpse and summoning branches of fire from the ground. From the tips of the bark came an army of fireflies of gold with talons and teeth sharp as a shark, but Yetzer, with a counter move, raised his arms with blazing flames from his hands, moving ever closer to rapidly burn the tree bark. The firelights flew to their death in a magical scene where holy light was on one side and the deathly flames of darkness was on the other. The closer he got, the more intense the fire, and the dead fireflies had been slayed. Lawrence didn't realize how close Yetzer had gotten since his flames were too bright. Eventually, he walked over to the dead god and broke each branch down, letting them fall to ash at the god's feet. Then Yetzer kicked the God of *Worlds* off the mountain, rolling off the steps at the bottom. He must have withstood several injuries to the point he had been deafened. He lay on his back, facing his father's sky. He wept. Though he was told his father wasn't ashamed, he still felt as though he had let his father down.

CHAPTER VI

HEALING BEIGE VERSUS BURNOUT SCARLET

The death phoenix floated down to his prey in a red haze, glowing of holiness, but it was only a costume. Here it seemed as if the god killer was going to show mercy for the very first time. He stood over the wounded entity and wished to have the same powers as him. He mustn't have thought about how even the evilest of beings can create and destroy. "What does mercy mean?" Yetzer had a general purpose.

Lawrence, with his last words, said, "Actions are reflections of one's soul. You out of all the beings in the universe could never show mercy." Yetzer had taken this as an insult, and he grabbed the legs of the demigod and then began to drag him to a dehydrated tree near the village on which he hung Lawrence in the shape of a *T*. His hands dangled, which caused his rings to fall next to his feet.

He said one last thing as he walked away. "I may not be able to show mercy but know that such an action always comes from somewhere. No being is born merciless." He had then set the tree on fire by placing his palm on the bark, where Lawrence had let out a loud cry. Then quietly, Death came to collect his soul, and shortly afterward, Lawrence's power soaked into the tree via his blood on the bark, then river-like to the roots, and finally, it grew into a plant which was edible.

Yetzer yanked the plant from the ground and munched on the spring demigod's power. It was such an awful title to hold to himself: the Devourer of Power. Death stood behind Yetzer in peril when Death had stood looking at the God of *Power*. Though Death should have said something, he didn't. He had to remember the foundation even if he was talking directly to calamity. With nothing to do, Death left and took Lawrence to the afterlife. Yetzer, in ancient antihero form, had finished eating the plant, and his skin where the lava flowed had glowed brighter. Once again, he looked powerful, and he felt powerful. His armor seemed to be integrated into his body, like a fusion between the Greek soldier set and his lava skin. His cape still hung just right at his shins at an angle, but where the clamps were to hold the cap, they seemed to be gone; and the fabric itself came out of his shoulder and hip. The God of *Power* had arrived in the same color red as his son. He had spoken first, "Yetzer, my demon child. Such great power has you. While our plan is running, there is more that needs to be conquered. We are not done yet. Keep up the work, and soon enough, this universe will be mine."

Yetzer wanted to hear something like a good job from his father, but it wasn't in him to say such a compliment. Yetzer had anger; his power glowed in such wrath. At what point was too much anger, where such a demigod would have to self-destruct or pass on the power? Either way, it wasn't a question Yetzer was asking himself. He held in his mind the idea and asked questions like

"I have power," "I need more power," "What does power mean?" and finally, "Am I in control of my power?" The God of *Power* had only two of these ideas in his mind, and as soon as he was about to lead Yetzer to the next demigod, Yetzer asked, "How much will it take for the universe to be ours?" He was stunned by why he used the word *ours,* for the God of *Power* had it in mind to be selfish. But he wouldn't tell his son this.

"Just enough for you to handle, my son." He ended the conversation with suspicion. The third planet from the sun was Yetzer's next destination, with a blue sky and green lands. Earth. The god of *Power* mentioned, "The next demigod you must eliminate next lives on a planet similar to yours. There are hills of sand with no powerful properties, but this planet also has a liquid you might find unfamiliar called water. Do try to stay clear away from it." Then he left in a ball of light once more, leaving his son alone, facing the Sapphire Summit. He thought of a world he could rule, but would it be under his father's control? So really it wouldn't be his rule.

Meanwhile on Earth, Zeno, the demigod of *Healing* had advanced quite rapidly with her healing abilities, though she could only heal herself and a few nearby creatures. She ultimately couldn't do a lot for the time being. The God of *Healing* had blended in with the rest of the planet. They both had traveled across this world, with each continent creating myths of their existence, but they weren't the only gods standing on Earth. The God of *Universal Travel* had also stayed on an adventure around the Earth. They would only meet once at a great wooden forest; this will later unfortunately become Bohemian Grove. Why was it that not just humanity but also gods who found this place a viable place to display their knowledge? Perhaps it was in the corner of the universe, or maybe it was just a coincidence. The two gods had seen each other in the blood-bark forest and exchanged words of greeting and hugs. "What brings you to this place, dear friend?" A question came from the God of *Healing*.

And in trying to not keep the conversation going, the God of *Universal Travel* responded, "Oh, you know. Just picking some weeds for a stew."

NIMMER

She was trying to be anonymous with her shy tone and fake smile. It wasn't known why she had been in that forest, but either way, it managed to be a good excuse. Sooner or later both gods disappeared from the location and never found their way back again. The God of *Healing* had other business to attend to, and the other god had showed up and then left with no reason. Zeno and her mother had started in the eastern part of the world. Some of the first civilizations recognized the gods that lived among them and wrote stories about them. The two primary legends were Gilgamesh and Beowulf—these first ideas of heroes and great evil. Of course, these stories came from the gods, and while the God of *Healing* had been more around the humans, Zeno hadn't. She didn't find humanity interesting. "Every human on this planet is worth less than the universe," he said once to his mother, who was too stunned to speak. She hadn't any idea of her son's values. It was unknown what he did value: objects or power. She did, however, take an interest in Death and how he was capable of keeping beings alive perhaps forever. To her, Death was the ultimate power.

Zeno didn't try anything new to conquer death; she did have the aspirations to gain more power. On one occasion, she found herself in a field, one she could call satisfactory; this was long ago. She was taking up a quest from monks in Egypt and following them across deserts to mountains to meditate. All the monks had the intention to find inner peace up in the mountains, but Zeno, with her somewhat hatred for humanity, had other intentions in persuading the monks to the mountains. They had walked from sand to snow; it had taken them a month to get to the desired destination. Zeno was up for the challenge; this trial was a good test for her ability to heal herself without any strain. She could heal both her exterior and interior, but she could only focus on one at a time. In this journey with the monks, she rarely ever got harmed, but when she did, either by thorns on a bush or blisters on her feet, she would quietly heal herself in a matter of seconds. Eventually, the monks would make it to the said mountain. Zeno stood on the edge of the mountain, taking in the dawn. Clear clouds sifted across the earth, the sun, with such glory, followed in its wake, and the earth itself was green holiness, the kind that was untouched by humanity.

Every monk called this place a sacred site to not only worship their god but to also become the ultimate individual thinker. The sun's love could only do so much, so as dusk fell on, the monks knew how to build a fire of orange and red. The leader of the monks said that they would get supplies and then each person would have to find a place of meditation. All understood this task, but Zeno had other plans. Of course, she wanted to meditate with the other monks, but she wasn't going to worship a god she never met. She was more interested in finding Death's lair. Zeno only saw the eyes of Death. She grew attached to him and the amount of "power" he held. She hated humans because in her mind, they weren't worthy of Death's royalty. To add more character to her, she wasn't going to kill the monks to make Death come to her, but she did think of it. She never grew attached to the monks she traveled with, so there wasn't much to lose. There was only one more woman and the rest were men who were older than twenty-eight years old. Though she wasn't ugly or the prime beauty, she was fairly gorgeous under the sun and moon.

With Yetzer's journey, he stayed on the planet Neptune for another day, exploring more of the planet and what the gods made with the village. He stayed on the outskirts of the village, watching how they behaved. He especially wanted to see how they would respond to their dead god. Nimmer reigned over the newly formed mountain and the staircase that ran up to the top. The dark-blue sand oozed on the ground like blood, mixing with normal blood from the two gods. On that night of revelation for the village, all was quiet.

The town's leader/priest had adventures outside of his home and walked to the tree where their beloved knight was hanged and burned. There was gore from the cold melted skin trapped inside the armor set. Only such an evil creature could cause such disgusting pain. The mortal holy figure stood blessing the corpse in the form of picking up the rings that still stayed on the ground, putting them on his heart, taking a deep breath, and then exhaling.

NIMMER

This was a tradition in the village where if a person passed, in order to bless the soul of the person, they would pick an item close to them and hold it dear to their heart while breathing and passing on loving energy to the fallen person. Yetzer had seen this action and couldn't understand why kindness was shown to the person he killed. In Yetzer's mind, in war, there were no sides. So to see a stranger choose love over his enemy, it stunned him. However, he kept watch on their actions; maybe he could learn to love by the sight of their hearts. The cleric walked back to the village. A crowd formed, and tears fell due to the incident of Lawrence's death. From Yetzer's eyes, he didn't gain anything from the sadness of others. With as much power he held, he still was a soulless creature. Shortly after their grief, they all came together to build a statue of green stone called the Knight of Neptune. They labeled this landmark as the capital, and when the sun's lights hit the stone, it glowed so that you could see it from space. The community had gasped in shock, for they had a beacon on their planet. That, too, seemed to draw in other planets.

Thus here began a tradition of trade and business with other planets across the universe. Shipping ports became more common, and after a few days, Yetzer was happily wasting time by sitting in the woods on the edge of the shade, seeing these aircraft fall from the sky and land to greet the natives of the planet, and a revolutionary economy rose. This, however, gave Zeno time to focus and prepare her powers of healing. Theoretically, she could be as powerful as the demigod of *Stars*. What's more powerful than being immortal? Eventually, Yetzer stopped his gaze upon the growing planet powerhouse and began his journey to Earth.

Moreover, back on Earth, Zeno had already claimed her spot, facing a pond inside a cave. Here, too, inside the cave, she had skulls and a depiction of witchcraft to, of course, spawn Death at her place of peace. At the age of twenty-three, she had been captured in headlights of the idea of Death falling in love with her. But she didn't want to eliminate herself from the world. She thought that if she could have a stronger sense of her healing capacity, she could then be in two places at once: the afterlife and mortal life.

NIMMER

Her witchcraft wouldn't be any use to her; magic rarely did any remarkable things for any demigod. It was purely raw power that buffed themselves.

Every day from dawn to noon, she got up from her flower bed and went forth a few feet away to her meditation spot. The sound of silence calmly guided her healing gifts to her brain, where her power recharged her to become more than before. The other monks had left her to her own business most days, but there was this unfortunate day when they all went down the mountain to gain food. Yetzer, however, had become closer to Earth as a tiny red light in the sky that lay back in front of the mountain. One of the monks had mentioned in a worrying note, "Has the scarlet light been in the sky for a long time?" They all had joined the monk in shaking nerve. Zeno, however, saw the light of Death and smiled. She had memorized the stars, and when she saw Yetzer's trail, she thought Death was finally coming for her love. However, when he showed up to her garden of witchcraft, she would know just what she spawned.

Yetzer flew past Mars and barely reached the atmosphere of Earth; he could smell the demigod. He, of all evil men, had a great sense of knowing where his enemies were. His light shined so beautifully that he had accomplished symbolizing Ares. Speaking of this god of war, the God of *Power* paid Asherah a visit in her white abode. She was sitting on her throne alone, not being visited by any of her creatures, not making any new creatures, and not doing anything on her behalf. The God of *Power* walked through the white steel front doors, which was odd considering they could spawn in the room with no need for walking. But to tell Asherah something was wrong, he walked in, presenting a question. "All time is yours, friend?"

Asherah was neutral with everyone; she never showed happiness or anger toward any of her fellow gods. She simply said with a tone of moralist intent, "Of course." With no follow-up remarks, it made the room go dim. Secretly the God of the *Power* had a hatred toward his creator.

He responded, "So what is it like to have your creations come and visit your kingdom?" he said this with intriguing clarity. He was the God of *Power*, but he wanted more—to ask Asherah about her time with such great power was part of his plan to conquer.

"Not many visitors often see their rightful home. I am here waiting for these days along these days."

This had been a good point to use to his advantage, "Do you visit your creations? Maybe they don't choose to follow your light because they don't know you reside here."

Asherah had enough of his existence in her kingdom, so as a closing statement while walking back to her throne, she said, "Dear friend, I am Providence. To whom would I prove myself? So good friends do visit me on more days."

The God of *Power*, though, wasn't done with the conversation. He angrily walked closer to her while she sat on her chair of royalty. "You are a lazy woman! To whom do you prove yourself? To me, the God of *Power*!" In a roaring voice, his eyes glowed red, the same to his own son's eyes of Death. He made it a point to make her feel scared and weaker than she presented herself.

"You shall not speak to me in a manner! I spawned alone in this universe and had to create your beings! What else must I go through to feel like such royalty!" In a loud stage presence, she yelled her surface emotions. She had the floor for this bit till the God of *Power* gave an unlikely promise to her.

"You're no god of mine. Someday soon I will gain enough power to eliminate you from your throne of shame. I may not carry sympathy within my heart, but I will never feel bad for where I came from." Then he walked out the same doors he came out of.

Asherah sat on her chair and shed a tear or two. She wasn't a malicious god; it was more of the fact that she wasn't qualified for such responsibility. To be everything to everyone had taken a toll on her and changed her own behavior in a way.

Now back on Earth, Yetzer had entered the atmosphere at dawn. He was at the base of the mountain where the grass he stepped on was burnt to ash. The very souls of his feet had heated the green to where it turned black. He and the all of unholy spirits in the universe had made every land he stood on cursed with his Nimmer. Zeno, unfortunately, with rose-colored lenses of love, set eyes on Yetzer. Here she truly believed that he was Death that she had summoned. He walked a few steps, then he lifted himself to where Zeno stood at the edge. Like Shakespeare's cinematic doomed romance, the two demigods had the impulsive intent to hold hands. Yetzer's hands were made of melting rock, so touching him would burn her, but she, the demigod of *Healing*, took the chance and stood in silence while burning alive and going in for a hug. It was an awkward but heartbreaking moment for Yetzer, though he stood six feet tall and appeared to be very intimidating. Once she hugged him, he knew two things that struck his mind: "All this time, all I needed was a hug" and "You are the demigod of *Healing*."

She asked his name. "Yetzer, Devourer of *Power*."

Zeno forcefully pulled away from Yetzer with an argumentative expression. "You are not Death?" She yelled then finally healed her skin from the brimstone.

"I am not, though it seems that I bring him with me everywhere I go." Zeno hadn't an idea what to do. Would she protect herself from this imposter of Death? Would she ask Yetzer to take her to Death? She walked away, back to her cave of worship to figure out how to bring Death to her. Yetzer followed behind her and told her his mission in a calm but malicious manner. "I've come to eliminate all the demigods in the universe for my father. You, my dear, will see Death one way or another."

She lit her candles and sat cross-legged while replying. "No, demon, that won't be necessary. I'll just try harder to connect to him my way." However, the Nimmer king wasn't planning on wasting time; just as she finished her statement and finally gave her guard up, Yetzer put her in a headlock while picking her up from the ground and holding her in a killing hug.

Glowing bright like an active volcano, he greatly scarred Zeno's back. She screamed but very quickly healed herself then broke out of the deadly hug. She ran further into the cave, hiding in the dark, almost tricking Yetzer into believing he was left alone. When she stayed in the dark for about a minute, Yetzer began to think she left. Yetzer was placed in between two symbolic shadows. The sun's light shone from outside of the cave. It was enough sight to find your way in, but for the rest of the cave where the sun's love didn't reach, it was a pitch-black cave that he had faced. He stared into the emptiness of the void, truly trying to figure out if she had left him alone in the cave, like when he was first born as a lonely being.

Yetzer explained to himself, "I am alone because the darkness can reach me." So he set flame to the cave where he stood. A burning light exposed Zeno and her hiding spot, and with quick thinking, Yetzer used his Nimmer to block the entrance to the cave. He made a wall of rock, trapping himself and Zeno within this room, and set it on fire. The healing demigod stepped over piles of fire, which eventually caused her to switch sides over to Yetzer, and he blended in within the fire. And the cracked wall had morphed into spikes on the wall for ambushing. Emerging out of the fire, Yetzer did exactly that, pushing Zeno into two spikes of amber and spearing her body, one through her side where her kidney was and in the middle of her chest but not penetrating the heart.

Her wounds turned black, and she screamed in agony. Her pain was too much for her healing. For she could not have focused on healing two of her wounds and her bare skin on fire. Yetzer stood in front of her in silence, almost as if he were a customer waiting in line. He displayed quietness within this moment of pure torture that he caused. His eyes didn't seem soulless, for they were full of the wrong light: the outer ring of the sun. He just had a bad father figure. Suddenly, Zeno had her moment of conversation with Yetzer. "There will be a time when you will forever be alone and engulfed in darkness."

He returned in his satanic, monstrous voice, "You see all this light I can make? I am who will never be alone again." From his hands, Yetzer slowly created a spike edging out of the wall, piercing Zeno's shoulder in seconds.

For her last words, she said, "You don't think for yourself do you?" The glimmer from Yetzer's face washed away. Lawrence had somewhat brought up this topic of thinking for himself.

"I don't think for the lives I take. I only think for myself when I am told." Death had emerged from the fire just as the final spike went through Zeno's heart of healing. A tentacle beam of beige spawned from her eyes, attaching to Yetzer's chest. He had absorbed her power of healing and became almost too close to a god. The room was in full bloom of scorching light. The cave had fallen in and the roof broke apart; part of it was melting and already breaking apart. A third of the roof fell to the floor, extinguishing some of the fire. The sky revealed the true sun's light; by this time, Yetzer had walked to a spot where no stone would fall on him. As the glory came to their faces, so did a romantic framework of Death and the demigod of *Healing*. "True healing is more than wounds on a body," Death said.

Helping her off the spike, Zeno replied, "True love isn't just for mortals." The black hooded figure had no effect whatsoever from the sun's light; he still presented himself as this existential figure even in the holy environments. Death took Zeno's soul by the hand, and they both danced within the rubble as two different-colored birds did to dance alongside their unusual beauty. All of this was happening without Yetzer's knowledge. He couldn't see Death or the souls he collected. He stood at the very same edge where Zeno stood before, overlooking and holding out his hands for his father. As the child of fire stood, the two star-crossed lovers vanished. Their story doesn't continue here.

The God of *Power* emerged from the sky with his voice of greatness. "One last demigod. Xanthia, the demigod of the *Stars*. Be not afraid of what she can do, they are mostly what you can do. But your flames come from a place greater than all the other worlds. Show her Nimmer is more powerful than a silly star formed by her father."

Upon the blue sky, Yetzer said, "Yes, Father. I shall tear the stars to shreds."

For the God of *Healing*, on the other hand, her whereabouts were unknown. Shamefully she wasn't aware of her daughter's journey with the monks. She stayed within the desert, and with time, she healed herself. Eventually, her name would be unknown to the world and universe, being famished and without a clue of where she could be on Earth. Though Death hadn't collected her soul, there would come a time when the God of *Healing* would reunite with her daughter.

CHAPTER VII

GLORIOUS GOLD VERSUS CRUSADE CARNAGE

*The s*eventeen-year-old blonde girl of the most powerful city in the universe was Xanthia, the demigod of Stars. Her home planet had partly been wasteland and lush forests. The city of Knox was primarily built with the ores of rose gold that gave a beautiful path at sunrise. When her father had killed the traitor a few weeks later, their empire grew to be the second most powerful planet in the entire universe, gaining more land and having an elite atmosphere. To them, they he*ld nu*mber one, but they didn't know anything about Nimmer, the planet of pure power. What the God of the Stars had was power and the very permission to create a star, but he was more political in the way of wanting to make sure that other planets knew of his name and his kingdom. What political power did to the kingdom *was* bearing a military force, but not one of the soldiers with guns. It had been made by the God of THE Stars to make mechanical weapons of explosions. "What better power is there than the kind that goes boom!" he rejoiced.

When this news came to Xanthia, she wasn't fond of the idea. She knew deep down when it came down to it, she'd have to be the only soldier on the field alongside her mother. She was someone she didn't want to be; both her parents trained her to be a walking death. At the end of the day where night was her only resting place, her sweat dripped off her face and into the ground to set a small smoke. What she wanted most of all to do with her hands was to paint. She loved painting the rose-gold buildings of her town and thought she found herself in art. She put her value in fighting with her hands. If those tanks and mechanical weapons of war failed, she was the runner-up in replacing the said golden army. The God of *Power* had changed personality when he first started building his empire; he seemed so wise and passionate about life.

Perhaps it was the challenges that came with not trying to be king, but in the end, he always was going to end up being royal. After his first kill of the rebel leader, he morphed from a friendly father to a frightening father, at least to his daughter. He went from wearing no crown and a clean and silk dark-blue button-up to now sporting a rose-gold crown, a white cloak, and white boots fit for royalty. He was a twisted Jack Frost for the sun instead of the winter. His wisdom had vanished, and he cared less and less about life except his own and his family's. He was never seen to act cruel to any living being, but it seemed that once he declared himself king, the power and control he gained must have altered his mind—an invisible form of corruption. What's a crown without deception? Xanthia's mother had devoted her life to being a soldier. It was perfect, especially for her rising kingdom. She held a symbolic position for war.

She desperately wished for Xanthia to be one with a blade, but she didn't find herself in weapons. Her light burned brighter with art, and her hands had been her weapons ever since she first used her powers of the sun. It was a curse, she first thought, when she had set fire to half of the world during the daytime, causing the half-desert, half-forest home planet. She was six years old when she set her world on fire. No one was killed in her awakening of the blooming sun, but once she realized her damage to her own planet, she let her tears fall, watering the ground where flowers of beige and pink had risen. Xanthia gave off radiant light, which was why the flowers grow so fast. She never held the idea of her being able to create pain and art at the same time, to burn the world with her hands but to also create flowers from her watered eyes. The very same light she used to destroy was used to create.

Xanthia's mother said to her daughter on her seventeenth birthday, "The light you hold is vastly stronger than you think, my child. Remember, to use light is to use the mind. Think wisely of what is worth putting in the dark." On the ending sunset of the day, they walked through the forest back to the kingdom where Xanthia's mother wanted to share more wisdom. They reached night skies by walking through the woods, "When in darkness, you must create your light." Putting her powers on display, she cast small dreams of fireflies in the air, lighting the area around them and captivating her mother in a beautiful painting of gold on the universe. They traveled further, getting closer to the doors, when suddenly out of the darkness were eight wolves of growling savage beasts. This wasn't part of any plan by the mother, so out of instinct, she said, "These creatures of the night aren't worthy of being in the light." Her meaning behind this was to make Xanthia think that not all living creatures deserve to live.

With quick thinking and slightly not paying attention to her mother's words, Xanthia raised her hands in the air, spawning the sun's light in her hands. It was not a flame and not falling lava but pure light in the palms, almost making it seem like it was daylight. It blinded the eyes of the mad dogs, casting them away from their path and making them weep away back to the shadows.

"No creature deserves to be taken away from the universe."

Fairly not impressed with her words, Xanthia's mother gave a side eye and then continued while hiding her true face. "Outstanding. Using light for good is well in your heart." She used a fake smile. They walked out of the grim trees and into their safe space of paradise. Xanthia felt encouraged when she used her light. This was her most important birthday.

The demigod of *Stars* had an even blend of both art and blade. For her mother's sake, she primarily put forth combat/training before her paintings. Wanting the best for her mother's wishes, she put her parents' needs before her own—a common trait she shared with Yetzer. However, she did think for herself, something Yetzer didn't do. Xanthia used her mind not just for combat; she thought of her own use to be one with her light. The more she did her paintings, the more she found wisdom in thinking for herself. Her eyes of low green sprang when she finally knew the difference between power of choice and power of force. Her wisdom of how to use violence came from her art, holding that perfect balance of art and blade.

The God of *Stars* was never going to fight for his kingdom. That was the point of the mechanism of war. He became twisted to the point where he saw both his female family members as only weapons. On the final days of the kingdom, where Yetzer was gliding through the universe on his way, the God of *Stars* had donned a purple pastor-like robe, black shoes, and gloves. Weirdly he was still wearing the rose-gold crown, a strange color palette. He was dressed in wealth and had no intention of partaking in the battlefield when the time came. He told his citizens that they were safe due to his presence of godly abilities, but he wouldn't be the one to lead an army or charge into war. He sat on his chair of misguided purpose, watching the sun rise and worshiping himself in a lust-brown hue. He called upon his army of metal when he saw a new star in his sky, a red blazing carnage fireball. Yetzer had been a day away from the God of *Star*'s eyes.

"Ready the armory! Close the doors! Prepare the people! Calamity has arrived!" He shouted to his staff of off-white robes, where six of them ran off in different directions. The queen (Xanthia's mother) had come out of her room to see the cause of this command.

"Has our time of reign come to an end?" she asked with teary eyes, and before the king could answer her question, down the hall, Xanthia had her power of true sun, engulfing her room in flames. She had spontaneously charged herself with energy in her sleep. The queen walked toward her daughter's room. Reaching out for the door, she opened it to a sight of the same power as when Xanthia first destroyed her world: the light of destruction.

With one breath from Xanthia's mouth, her room blew up. Every art piece she made turned into ashes, her gowns of rose gold rusted to smithereens, and her detonation created a nova of carnage, practically destroying her entire kingdom over again. The queen was too close to her daughter's blast to survive; as she opened the door, Death emerged from the other side. She couldn't react fast enough to her daughter's sailor burst, and so she disintegrated in a matter of seconds. As she died, Death had given the soldier a hug while they both stood impenetrable.

NIMMER

It was not just Xanthia's room but also her royal building that came down as the flames grew with her multicolored solar burst. These bursts of hers came in waves of three. The first one killed her mother, destroyed her room, and tore down the kingdom. The second one had leveled the building, losing the God of *Power* in the rubble.

The third burst had history repeating itself. She set her world on fire once more; this time, as the tanks were starting to roll out, it had seemed that a nuclear explosion had occurred. On Xanthia's last blast, she collapsed her world, burning everything with her light. From Yetzer's point of view on the outskirts of the atmosphere, he had seen a giant explosion, and he first thought, *Has someone beat me to the demigod?* With this question in his mind, he had this determination to find the one who took his place. In perfect timing, Xanthia finally woke up from her explosion slumber. Her eyes opened to no roof and no walls, nothing but rubble of rose-gold bricks and glass. The tanks were a few miles away from her bed, and with those war machines out, Xanthia knew that calamity had arrived.

She got out of bed and looked around for her parents, and where her door was, she noticed her mother's arm. She moved the door to reveal her broken mother with a smashed face, and half of her body was gone, turned into dust. Just then, Yetzer entered the world with a loud boom, and the tanks were commanded to shoot at any incoming entity. And Yetzer swirled around the sky, dodging these war bullets. With the loud booms, Xanthia knew she only had a matter of minutes before calamity began to look for her. She didn't bother looking for her father. He didn't care for her well-being, and neither did she. Xanthia, using her light for one final peaceful moment, carried her mother to a nearby forest that was fairly near her room. Placing the body on the grass, she cried as much as she could. She used all her water within her soul to grow a moss-willow tree from her dead mother's heart, with her radiant light the tree grew to be the biggest lifeform in the world. When it finished growing, she stood to worship her achievement in life.

With dark-blue and mistic-red flaming hair and with the combination of pride, death, and anger, she went to kill this calamity, and if not to eliminate then to warn. As the two demigods were a mile away, walking toward each other, Yetzer had taken a good look at where the tanks were, and they seemed to be lined up at the edge of the ruined kingdom. He stopped in the air and used his Nimmer from his hands to strike a ball of cosmic matter that deteriorated the metal of the tanks. He had destroyed two out of the seven tanks. He landed on the ground, kneeling on the orange sand of acceptance. He felt the sand, and to him, it was like going to a country where they spoke your language but you couldn't understand what they were saying. Gripping the understanding of his existence in this world, he said, "Will I be defeated here?" He recognized the texture of the sand but couldn't do anything with it. No advantages came with the environment he stood in. He made it a plan not to be destroyed by another demigod's hands, but he accepted that he might not complete his mission.

Moments later the rest of the tanks blasted their bullets at the demigod of fire, and he charged Nimmer and crusaded forward, in this cinematic case of rapid firepower targeting this one entity on orange sand and him walking forward and taking these incoming forces. He was a man of immunity. It seemed as if he continued with no resistance; he had this symbol on his shoulders of crusade carnage. On the other side, behind the tanks and just a few feet away, Xanthia continued walking too, unknown to Yetzer's knowledge due to the size of the tanks being in the way. Just as Xanthia got tired of the tanks due to their uselessness, Yetzer flew in the air to strike once more; but this time, instead of his usual defensive, he used his Nimmer of flame to melt the metal. And from the sky, a river of fire fell onto the war machines. Yetzer landed back on the ground and, with perfect timing, exited the fire. Then came the sight of Xanthia and her rightful royalty. Yetzer stood in silence and stared at Xanthia and her beloved power of light. Her confidence in her eyes of gold beamed like the yellow brick road. Xanthia had set herself on fire. She became a waking inferno; from her head going down to her feet, she was consumed in the flame of cosmic rays. It was a different form of fire than Yetzer.

He was the child of fire, and she was the child of light. The fire practically came off her skin and caused her own aura to have a strong tint of blue flame, a sense of pride. The bloom of her power grew beyond what Yetzer had in store within himself. Once that blue firewall came up, Yetzer knew he had to get more power before he could even draw blood from the demigod of the *Stars*. Xanthia broke the silence. "Your soul will land in my hands if you come this way. I hold the power of a star. You, calamity, I do not fear."

Yetzer's hands didn't flinch or shake; they remained with the power of Nimmer. His face shifted from a smirk with power to annoyance with doom. He thought that maybe she was lying, but her power was on display. So he considered taking a step back. Just then, Yetzer's father had whispered in his ear without being seen. "Leave her. Come back to Nimmer. The plan is finished."

Yetzer had seemed disappointed in his father's reaction. With a final ending for the demigods' meeting, Yetzer said, "All forms of light will come to an end, starting with you."

CHAPTER VIII

POWER OVER FAITH

An eruption from the sand followed Yetzer's feet as he left. He accepted his fate of being not worthy of a cosmic fight. For Xanthia, her existence stayed on her newly named planet Luz Central. While her planet was empty and she was the only being on site, she didn't let the loneliness get to her mind. Such a darkness can cause an entity to turn to evil. Instead, she once more used her light to spawn new life on her own planet, and this time she'd be better than her missing father. Xanthia looked everywhere for her father's existence, but any trace of him was gone except for the rose-gold crown that was left forgotten by the accepting sand. He had left the spot he was in under the rubble when the kingdom collapsed. Xanthia hadn't any more emotions for her father. With his disappearance, she carried on with the light.

The shameful god was more cowardly than any lion for leaving his daughter. With her whole planet being of sand, she took light from the sun to grow grass of wisdom. Here she pushed the boundaries of being two gods in one, terraforming her entire planet with her hands. From her champion gesticulation, this is where her story ends but also starts.

Now Yetzer's eyes were set on his home planet, maybe to gain more power. He had this final question for himself, "Do I think for myself?" Drifting in the cosmos, his eyes watered, for he hadn't found the true answer for his mind. His mind began to crack like a tombstone in hurricane weather. The idea of him having open-mindedness had torn apart his power. This happened to the point where it had seemed as if he gained consciousness. His eyes widened in new purpose and color; rather than his original carmine red, it had changed to a dark tangerine.

The God of *Power* waited for his son on Nimmer, out in the open dark sand, his son's birthplace. His gown was dark blue and had blended with the sand, as if he had risen from the ground. It was the perfect symbolism for pride and death and not the purple corruption, because you can't corrupt something that was never good. He gave birth to this demon child. Now he was going to take his child out of the universe. Yetzer hadn't any idea of this part of the plan, even in his grand awakening while flying between the stars. The God of *Power* had touched the sand of Nimmer, and just like with Yetzer and the orange sand, he, too, felt as if he spoke the language but didn't understand what was being said. "Useless oil," the God of *Power* said then, letting go of the midnight-blue substance.

Entering the atmosphere in unholy prophecy, a glow of death, and the divine fire, his cape flared and his hands gave an offer, set on scarlet flame. The dark child felt at home when standing once more on his harnessed power of Nimmer-Blue. Yetzer, kneeling before his creator, said, "Father, to have power is to have faith."

The God of *Power* had responded to his son's joyous statement, "To have faith is to believe there is someone above yourself, and no one in this universe shall have more power than me." The profound, corrupted god then put his hands on his son's chin, lifting him from the ground and taking a solid two minutes examining Yetzer's gear.

Now with an open mind, Yetzer asked, "Wouldn't God herself be more powerful than you?"

Coming back around and meeting his eyes, the God of *Power* now mentioned his despicable plan. "That is where you come in, my child. I will take your power to kill the ruling entity and become a new God."

Here, Yetzer began to somewhat panic. With his ideas of maybe dying in the process even if his father didn't say it in his own words, he felt that this was the end for him. At Yetzer's sacrifice, the God of *Power* would become a new God, and it would be true to what his plan was. If the God of *Power* were able to gain his son's power, he would be able to kill God herself. Yetzer took a step back and set his hands on fire as a defense, but his father did not want to lose any more time. The God of *Power* was able to lift Yetzer in the air via telekinesis control over the power within Yetzer. Yetzer was held in a sort of biblical arrangement, with his arms being pulled and his legs dangled over the Nimmer sand.

Yetzer had screamed and pleaded with his father. "Please, Father! I'm alive! I'm alive! I'm alive!" With malicious eyes and the grip of torture, the God of *Power* responded with a question, "Sure you're alive, but are you conscious?" And with no response, slowly and painfully Yetzer's power was being drained from his body. Dark-blue sand particles came out from his skin, and he was being dismantled before his father's eyes.

In Yetzer's upcoming death, instead of his father taking all this power for himself, Yetzer chose to self-destruct. There was a rumbling from his chest, then colors of death tore through the skin of the demigod. The God of *Power* thought that his plan was working and that finally he would be the most feared one in the universe, but this was far from something to gain. The very same gold-pink lemonade hue shined his face, and here, one final time, he felt true happiness. "I shall tear open the universe!" were the last words from the child of fire. His cursed words and the explosion of his body ripped a hole in the universe, causing a bright light and changing the sand from dark blue to a dissolving pink. It was entering holy love, but it was running out.

Death hadn't shown up to collect Yetzer's soul due to the demigod having too much power and therefore not having room for a soul. After the blindness from the light had gone away, the God of *Power* set his sights upon the new beings not from his universe. They were the biblical angels Virtues, Dominions, and Principalities. "Which source caused our existence to travel?" Virtues said.

The God of *Power* spoke to the entities. "The light from my son has brought you here. You beings might not have power, by any chance?" He was a sobbing father at first, then he morphed into the sinful god he was.

Principalities spoke a fact to the God of *Power*. "If power is all that you crave, then you will eventually run out of room for a soul."

There was a silent moment, then came the realization from Dominions, who told the other angels, "This is not our place of worship or governance." They turned their heads in all directions to view their place of Nimmer.

Virtues had walked away from the two angels, its light dragging across Nimmer as if clearing water, then he said, "This faith of ours must be held in mind in time when not in the saint's home." An idea came from Dominions with his tools of royalty. He suggested that he use his seal of God to find the creator of this universe to see if she could help them find their way home. However, when the God of *Power* listened to the word *faith*, he stood in the angels way.

"This universe has not any idea of angelic royalty. Here it's power over faith."

The angel Principalities then created a being from the Nimmer they floated above. Rather than a child of demonic spawn, this new being of Nimmer would spread the faith of the angels. "Child of faith, rise and redeem to collect dreams, guide us through the universe by your power to saith, and save us from this paucity of faith." Principalities had whispered into her palm then grabbed a chuck of the Nimmer. The words of the angel's light had powers of creation.

Rising from the dark-blue sand stood a boy of fairly light blue, a human but not one of earth, a boy of faith created by the angel's light. Virtues had given the child the nickname Mr. Sandman, the child of faith and dreams. He seemed to be born with more wisdom than an average creature.

A word from the wise, dear reader: "Pain must come before love. Pain builds and strengthens your powers to heal yourself. Know that your love is never a weakness, and to have love in any form is a gift. To have power is to have faith. You have a mind to think for yourself. To use light is to use the mind. Think wisely of what is worth putting in the dark. Always remember, you are not alone."

The End
To be continued.

ABOUT THE AUTHOR

Romeo Vega is a Boricua on his dad's side, and one of his goals is to show the family that he not only can write a good story but also inspire anyone who wants to create something and dare to call it art, either in the form of writing a book or building a small sculpture for a project in school. He is hoping one day to tell his father that he is his rising sun and that he carries all of his family and will always be willing to. He used to think fashion was his calling for a long time but now doesn't feel connected to it anymore. In his mind, it was too gay for him, so that led to him drifting away from it because he didn't want to rely on his sexuality to dictate his personality.